Best Friends Forever

First Edition, 2018

ISBN: 9781980581895

Jay Argent
jay@jayargent.com

www.jayargent.com

Best Friends Forever

Jay Argent

Prologue

Dark clouds covered the sky, and the first raindrops wet the t-shirts of the two fourteen-year-old boys who rushed under a tall white oak. Side by side, they curled up on the ground, their backs against the trunk of the tree. Unfortunately, the sprawling leaves gave them hardly any shelter against the increasing wind and rain.

"Aw, man. My shirt is all wet," Matthew said, shielding his face with his hands.

Ignoring the heavy rain, Liam stared at the boy's white t-shirt, which had become transparent. Under it, Matthew's chest moved up and down as he breathed. Liam shifted his gaze to Matthew's shorts and then to his legs, which were touching Liam's. On their feet, they had similar blue sneakers; Liam had begged his mom to buy them as soon as he had seen Matthew wearing his.

"We better leave. The rain might not stop for a long time," Matthew said as he stood. He offered Liam his hand to pull him up.

Matthew's wet shirt was hugging his upper body when he walked in front of Liam, who couldn't keep his eyes away from his friend's back. Soon, they reached their bikes, which they had left leaning against a massive rock when they went to check if there were any birds on the lake. Matthew suggested they ride to his house, which sounded good to Liam.

The boys were neighbors, and their families lived in the countryside, some miles north of Grand Rapids, which meant that Liam didn't have to share his best friend with anyone. Liam was an only child, and Matthew's sister, who was two years older, seldom showed any interest in what the boys were doing.

"Go to the bathroom," Mrs. Evans ordered when she saw the two soaked boys opening the front door.

Liam gave Matthew's mother a shy nod and followed his friend down the hall, hoping his muddy sneakers wouldn't leave marks on the floor. He took even longer and more careful steps after he heard a heavy sigh behind his back.

"Take off your wet clothes." Her voice came from the living room.

Liam began to untie his shoes, dawdling as much as he could. The wet shirt was uncomfortable, but the idea of taking it off made him feel self-conscious. He glanced at Matthew, who had already removed his shirt and was unzipping his shorts. Soon, his friend was standing there in only his wet underpants. Liam eyed him one more time.

"Liam, do you need help with your shoes?" Mrs. Evans asked. Her voice was as toneless as usual, and she was holding a pile of dry clothes.

"Um … no, I'm okay," Liam said and looked around.

"Matthew, here's a towel for you. Go to your room to change your clothes," Mrs. Evans said. "Liam, you can get dressed here," she added and set the clothes and a big towel on the table.

Only when he was alone did Liam take off his wet clothes and use the towel to dry himself. *These are Matthew's clothes*, he thought when he put on the light blue underpants, brown shorts, and white t-shirt, all of which were too loose for him.

"I called your mother. You can wait here until it stops raining. I'll make dinner soon," Mrs. Evans said when Liam came out of the bathroom.

Liam thanked her and climbed the stairs to Matthew's second-floor bedroom. His friend was already waiting for him there, holding a board game on his lap. They had played Carcassonne multiple times at the school library, but the box that Matthew was carrying was a birthday present from Liam.

"Do you want to play?" Matthew asked as he started opening the box.

"Of course," Liam said and sat on the floor next to Matthew.

"Or should we take a couple rounds of Twister?" Matthew said and turned to look at Liam. "Maybe Maria will let us borrow it."

"Let's ask."

Matthew put the game box back on a shelf, which was full of Legos and board games. He gave Liam a coy smile and pushed his friend into the hall. Maria was reading on her bed, but she put the book on the nightstand when the boys stopped at the door.

"Can we borrow your Twister?" Matthew asked.

"You want to play it, too?" she asked Liam.

Feeling fluttering in his belly, Liam nodded quickly, and his eyes grew bigger. He watched Maria taking the game from the drawer and opening the box. "This time I'll beat you," Liam said, poking Matthew's chest.

"In your dreams," Matthew said. He wrapped his arm around Liam's head and forced him down on the floor.

"Boys, stop. Maybe I should play with Liam." Maria said. "Matthew, you can spin the spinner."

Matthew let go of Liam, and both of them looked at Maria. A wave of disappointment went through Liam's body when Matthew shrugged and sat on the bed. Maria gave her brother the spinner and began spreading the mat on the floor. Liam stared at his friend, but it didn't help; Matthew just held the spinner in his hands, avoiding his gaze. Finally, Liam gave up and took his position on the edge of the mat.

"Right hand, red," Matthew said.

Liam waited until Maria had chosen a circle on the mat before he laid his hand on the closest red circle. Matthew kept calling out moves, and Maria came closer and closer to Liam, who had stayed on his side of the map. After the next move, Maria's leg rested on Liam's back. He tried to move farther so that Maria wouldn't be touching him, but he fell to the ground.

"Wow, that was quick!" Maria said and did a victory dance on the floor.

Liam shook his head. "Whatever you say."

"Okay, who wants to play with me?" Matthew said and looked at Liam.

"Me," Liam said and jumped to the edge of the mat.

It was Maria's turn to use the spinner, and the boys took positions on the map, trying to block each other. Soon, Matthew ran out of options, and he had to shift his leg over Liam to reach a yellow circle. The next moved forced him to place his hand over Liam, who was now below him. Liam raised his body so that his back touched Matthew's chest.

"That's not fair!" Matthew protested, trying to find a better balance.

"Don't spin yet. Let's see how long he can keep that position," Liam said and raised himself even higher.

"I'm not giving up," Matthew said, resting his weight on Liam.

Liam tensed his hands and legs not to fall. Matthew felt heavy on his back, but he felt good, too. Suddenly, Matthew stopped playing the game and wrapped his arms and legs around Liam. As soon as he began tickling Liam, they collapsed on the floor. Matthew didn't let go of his friend, who giggled and fought to break free.

"Stop!" Liam gasped. "Please!"

"Not before you admit that I won."

"Never."

Their wrestling was interrupted by Mrs. Evans' voice calling that it was dinner time. The boys stood up, and Liam tucked in his shirt. He hoped that Maria would leave the game on the floor so they could continue playing it later. Unfortunately, she didn't.

"God, we thank you for this food," Mrs. Evans said after everybody had sat around the table.

Liam kept glancing at Matthew, trying not to laugh, as Matthew's mom continued the blessing. Having heard her say it several times, it still sounded funny. Matthew's cheeks were flushed, and Liam shifted his focus to his empty plate, trying to avoid embarrassing his friend more. Obediently, he waited until Mrs. Evans had thanked God for pretty much everything.

The rain had stopped by the time they finished dinner, and Mrs. Evans suggested it was time for Liam to go home. Matthew walked him to the front yard where they had left their bikes. Liam lingered, thinking of something to do or say.

"Should I come to your house tomorrow," Matthew asked, "after we get home from church?"

"Great, I can sleep late," Liam said.

"Wish I was that lucky." Matthew watched as Liam disappeared behind the tall fence.

A couple hours later, Liam was in his bed reading a book, but his mind was continually wandering to high school, which would begin next week. He hoped the teachers would be nice and he would have some classes with Matthew. School wasn't, however, the only thing that concerned him. Denying his growing feelings for his best friend was getting harder and harder.

I think I'm gay, Liam thought. It wasn't something he could tell Matthew, or anybody. He just hoped Matthew would be his best friend forever and things would sort out somehow.

Their teachers turned out to be nice, and Matthew sat next to him in every class, but their friendship lasted only until the end of their freshman year, when Matthew suddenly disappeared from his life.

A week after the school year had finished, a big red moving van took away his friend and the entire family. It all happened out of the blue. No early warning, no goodbyes, nothing. One day, Matthew was gone, and Liam never heard from him again.

Chapter 1

TODAY

"Um ... you need to stop it," Alex said, trying to focus on driving.

"Say it," Liam teased and kept stroking Alex's boner through his shorts.

Alex was silent for a moment. Then his face twisted into a grimace, and his breathing became faster. "Okay, okay. You won."

"Here's the winner," Liam proclaimed and pulled his hand off his boyfriend's crotch. "I knew you couldn't take it."

Alex mumbled something and fixed his shorts. Only a few miles were left before they would arrive in Fairmont. After a long trip from Eddington, Liam was excited to see his parents for the first time in several months. Mom and Dad had visited him on campus soon after he had been kidnapped and Tyler had died, and they had left only after Liam had promised to call them every night.

They passed their old high school, and Liam saw the empty parking lot. Like many times when Alex had driven him home from school, Liam took hold of Alex's hand. It had been their thing. Two boys, unlikely friends, sharing a big secret they tried to hide from the rest of the world. Alex squeezed his hand.

"Do you think you might see some of your old teammates tomorrow?" Liam asked.

"Seniors just graduated. I don't think I know many of the younger kids," Alex replied.

"It was very nice of Coach Hanson to offer you that job."

Alex flashed a smile at Liam. "I can hardly wait to get back in the pool."

They crossed the bridge over the river and turned right to the suburb where Liam's parents lived. There were familiar buildings on both sides of the street, and then they saw the white house. Liam's mother was sitting on the terrace reading a book, but as soon as she saw Alex's red Mustang, she stood up and rushed to the gate.

"Come here! I want to hug you both," she shouted.

Liam smiled at her enthusiasm but followed the order, as did Alex. Soon Liam's father appeared in the yard, greeted the boys, and helped Alex carry their luggage into the house. Meanwhile, Liam and his mother walked farther from them. When they stopped by the old apple tree, her face grew severe.

"Is he still depressed?" she asked.

"I think he's getting over it," Liam said. "At least, he seems to be excited about the swimming camp."

"He isn't blaming himself anymore for what happened?"

"Alex will always believe it's his fault if anything bad happens."

She put her hand on Liam's shoulder. "Give him some time."

In spite of the huge amount of clothes Liam had packed, Alex and Mr. Green got the car unloaded quickly, and all of them gathered in the kitchen. Having driven several hours, the boys were hungry, especially Alex, who had been waiting for Mrs. Green's delicious cooking. His mother, now deceased, had never excelled in that domain.

"So, you'll start coaching the high school swim team tomorrow," Mrs. Green said to Alex.

"Yes. They have a camp in Buonas," Alex said. "The coach called me and asked if I could help."

"Oh. That's nice. You were always his star swimmer," she said.

While the compliment made Alex beam, Liam caught his mother's eye. *Damn it, Mom. Don't screw this up*, he thought and signaled with eyebrows. She nodded and changed the topic quickly. Liam relaxed only after he had stolen a glance at Alex, who seemed happy and was eating with a good appetite.

When they got to dessert, Liam told his parents about his new job at a coffeehouse in Eddington. The owner had agreed to let him start in two weeks, after swim camp ended. Unfortunately, Alex would be spending those two weeks in Buonas, which meant they wouldn't have much time to see each other before returning to Eddington. Luckily, Liam's father had a solution to keep Liam busy.

"The garbage company is bringing a dumpster tomorrow morning," Mr. Green said.

"Please don't say they're coming early," Liam groaned and noticed both his parents nodding.

"We thought you could start by cleaning the attic," she said.

"Fabulous," Liam said, rolling his eyes.

After dinner, Alex and Liam drove to the church and walked to the nearby graveyard where Alex's mother was buried. Alex stared at the stone silently with Liam's arm wrapped around him. The grass was long, and nobody had brought flowers. Liam wished they had bought some on their way there.

"Dad doesn't care," Alex said. "What a surprise."

Liam looked at Alex and noticed his teary eyes. Feeling a lump in his throat, he tried to find something to comfort his boyfriend, but nothing came out of his mouth. Alex kneeled and began to clean the front of the grave. He ripped away the overgrown grass with his hands to reveal the text written on the stone.

"If she had had more time, she would have accepted … us," Liam said.

"I don't know. I'll just be happy when we get back to Eddington."

Alex looked sad. He had the same empty gaze in his eyes he'd had for weeks after Tyler's death. It worried Liam. *Maybe swim camp isn't the best idea*, he thought and pursed his lips.

"Of course it's nice to see your parents," Alex said quickly when Liam was silent. "It's just that everything else here reminds me of my fucked-up parents."

Liam hugged his boyfriend, and they kissed. One thing led to another, and soon Liam found his hand inside Alex's shorts. They looked at each other; both of them had smiles on their faces. *He's so handsome*, Liam thought and kissed Alex one more time.

"Um … isn't this a little inappropriate here?" Alex said.

"Let's go home," Liam said.

"But your parents are there."

"I'm sure Mom will let us keep the bedroom door closed."

"You're awful."

"Says the one who has a boner in the graveyard."

Alex drove through the center of Fairmont because they wanted to see if their old hometown had changed while they had been gone. It hadn't. They saw the park where Alex had spent time with his friends and the old mall where Liam's mother worked and where they'd almost had their first date. Neither of them said anything when they passed the place where Sam had tried to kill Liam.

Fairmont was full of memories, and some of them were better than others. It was where they had met and fallen in love with each other, but neither of them wanted to move back there after graduation.

It was getting dark when Alex parked his car in front of the house. They went in and found Liam's parents watching television in the living room.

"You want to join us? The movie's starting soon," Liam's mother said.

"Nah. We're going to my room," Liam said.

Liam closed the bedroom door behind him and laughed when he heard the volume of the television being increased. *How thoughtful of them*, he thought and wrapped his arms around Alex. They hugged and kissed, and in no time, Liam had stripped off all his boyfriend's clothes.

Alex was standing naked in front of him. His erection was pointing up toward the ceiling—and, most importantly, he had a sexy smile on his face. For months, Liam had been watching his sad, glassy eyes. He was happy to get his boyfriend back.

"Please fuck me," Alex whispered shyly in Liam's ear.

Liam kissed his boyfriend, who had blushed slightly. "My pleasure," he said and felt how blood flew down to his crotch.

Alex lay down on the bed Liam's mother had made for them. The silky linens were soft and smelled fresh. Liam took off his jeans and pulled a condom and lube from his bag. Then he joined his boyfriend on the bed.

Alex moaned softly when Liam moved his hand along his back toward his butt.

"You're so sexy," Liam whispered and grabbed Alex's buttock.

Liam checked one more time that the door was closed and then he moved on top of Alex. Their bodies were pressed together, and Liam felt Alex moving slowly under him, trying to get even closer to him. Liam wrapped his arms around Alex's chest and lowered his head on Alex's shoulder to kiss his cheek.

"Are you ready?" Liam whispered.

Alex nodded and closed his eyes. Slowly and gently, Liam entered his boyfriend, who had a hard time staying silent. They stayed like that for a while, enjoying the intimacy of the moment, before Liam started to move his body carefully. His motions were calm, but he felt how Alex tensed under him, and his breathing became heavier.

"I'm gonna cum," Alex panted in a low voice.

"Do it," Liam whispered and pushed his lower body against Alex.

They both came, Alex first and Liam soon after him. They both wore wide smiles as they lay on the bed, Liam using Alex's shoulder as a pillow. Finally, Liam rose to get some tissues from the table. He gave them to Alex, who sat up.

"Holy shit, what a mess," Alex said when he saw the bed under him.

"Let's turn the blanket around," Liam said. "And that's definitely your side of the bed," he added.

Alex didn't have time to protest before they heard a voice from the kitchen. "Boys, would you still like to eat something?"

"Just a second, Mom!" Liam shouted, and they began to put their clothes on.

Early the following morning, Alex was in his car, on his way to Buonas. The previous night with Liam's parents had been fun, and it was a pity he had to leave so soon, but Alex had promised to help Coach Hanson at swim camp. The participants would be the kids on the Fairmont High School swim team except the seniors who had already graduated.

Maybe I could become a teacher, Alex thought. Liam was a history major, so perhaps they could work at the same school. Liam would be a great history teacher, and Alex could teach math and coach the swim team. Alex made a mental note to talk to the college counselor about his options.

Alex followed the signs to the Green Park Swim Center. It was in a rural area twenty miles north of Buonas, famous for its outdoor pool. Memories of his high school time filled his mind when he saw the familiar buildings. *Rick and I slept in that cottage, and we were still friends*, he thought when he passed the lodging area before parking his car closer to the pool.

Nothing had changed. The parking lot, all the signs, and the white main building were exactly as they had been when Alex had last visited the center. At the back of the yard, there was even the ramshackle storage shed behind which he and Sam had smoked. Or, to be precise, Sam had smoked, and he had kept watch so the coach wouldn't see them.

Speak of the devil, Coach Hanson came out of the door, and a warm smile appeared on his face when he saw Alex. "Alex, welcome to Green Park," he shouted.

"Thanks. It's been a while. Are the kids here already?" Alex asked.

"Waiting for you at the auditorium," Coach Hanson said with a meaningful look at his watch.

"Oh, I didn't—" Alex began to say, but the coach interrupted him.

"How're you? Are you and Liam still together?"

"Huh? Yeah … we share a dorm room, and our studies are progressing well."

The old man stared at Alex, who looked down and crossed his arms. They went inside the building but stopped at the hall, which was empty. The sound of loud conversation came from the auditorium, which was on the left.

"Have you seen your father?" Coach Hanson asked.

Alex shook his head. "He's not okay with me…."

"I've tried to talk to him, but he doesn't want to see me."

Coach Hanson and Alex's father were old college friends. The coach had helped Dad when Alex's mother had died, but then alcohol and some unexplained bitterness had started playing a more prominent role in Dad's life, and he had finally secluded himself.

"Thanks, but I need to accept the fact that I don't have a dad anymore," Alex said. "Or a mother."

"Sorry, kid. Life is cruel sometimes," the coach said. "Let's go," he added and patted Alex on his shoulder.

There were twenty high school boys in the auditorium, enthusiastically chattering. They took their seats as soon as Coach Hanson walked in. Alex followed him to the podium and scanned the room. He recognized some of the faces, but most of the boys were new to him, which wasn't a surprise. Two classes of seniors had graduated since he had been on the team.

"This is Alex. He'll be the other coach here," Coach Hanson said. "He's a former student of Fairmont High and one of the best swimmers we've had."

Everybody in the room stared at Alex, who didn't know if he should have said something. Alex glanced at the coach and raised his hand a bit to greet the students. Scratching the back of his neck, he opened his mouth to introduce himself, but Coach Hanson continued speaking before any words came out.

Ten minutes later, everybody knew the rules of the camp: wake-up at half past six, no smoking, no alcohol, no phones during practices, and curfew at ten. Alex recalled how the coach had sent Sam home from their first camp after he had been late to morning practice for the third time in a row.

"Right side of the room, you ten, follow me," Coach Hanson said. "The rest of you stay here, and Alex will explain today's schedule," he added and gave Alex a wrinkled piece of paper.

Alex studied the paper and waited until half the boys had left the auditorium. Then he put the paper on the table and his hands on his pockets. Two of the boys in the back row were whispering something to each other; the front row was silent and looked at him.

"Um … like you heard, I'm Alex," he said. "Alex Wesley," he added. His cheeks felt hot. All the students were looking at him.

"There are some rumors," a tall boy in the back row said. His face looked familiar, and Alex was rather sure his name was Roy. The boy continued, "We heard you like naked guys."

The other boy in the back row laughed. The front row was silent and waited to see Alex's reaction. *I should've seen this coming*, Alex thought and tried to figure out the best way to respond. He just stood there, his entire face and neck as red as a firetruck.

"Yes. I'm gay," Alex said finally. "But you don't need to worry. I'm not going to…."

His voice trailed off. *I don't owe them an apology for being gay*, Alex realized. He took the paper from the table and straightened up. He read the schedule calmly in a loud voice and asked the boys to follow him to the locker room. They walked after him, Roy and his friend behind the others.

The locker room was a square. Lockers lined three walls, and the shower room was located on the other side of the aisle. Alex chose the first locker on the right and took his speedo from the bag. He took off his shirt and was about to remove his pants when Roy interrupted him.

"Are we supposed to change our clothes here?" Roy said.

"Well, this is the locker room," Alex said. "What's the problem?"

"You."

Roy was standing with his arms crossed in the middle of the room. His friend from the back seat was on his left side. The other boys were sitting on the benches in front of the lockers. Some of them were looking at Alex, while some had their heads down.

This is ridiculous. I need to end this shit now, Alex thought and walked up to Roy. Their heads were barely ten inches from each other, but Roy didn't budge.

"I'll be coaching you the next two weeks, whether you like it or not," Alex snapped. "Now, suit up."

"Not until you leave," Roy said and mouthed "faggot" to emphasize his statement.

"I'm not going anywhere," Alex said.

"As you can see," Roy said, looking at the other boys, "the homo wants to see us naked." Some of the boys laughed.

The smirk on Roy's face made Alex's blood boil. He glared at Roy, pointing at him with his finger, but said nothing. *I should be the adult here*, Alex reminded himself and returned to his locker. He continued changing his clothes and ignored Roy, hoping the boys would follow his example. They didn't, and soon Alex was the only one in the room wearing a speedo.

"What's taking so long?" Coach Hanson roared when he entered the locker room.

"But, he's—" Roy began to say.

"If you want my support for your scholarship application, you'd better be in the pool already," Coach Hanson interrupted him.

All the boys began undressing immediately, even Roy. In less than a minute, they were wearing their swimming trunks and were ready for practice. Alex felt relieved but humiliated that the coach had to save him. He hoped the rest of the day would go better, but he wasn't too optimistic that would be the case.

This will be a long two weeks, Alex thought as he led the boys to the pool.

The attic was full of brown cardboard boxes piled side by side. On top of them were plastic bags filled with old clothes Liam's dad had packed. One corner held a collection of suitcases beside a huge vase. A bit farther from them was a pile of roof tiles and a roll of fiberglass insulation. It was hard to believe they had lived there only three years.

Sunlight came through the small window on the east side wall and shed light on an old bicycle. Liam picked it up and wiped the dust from the seat. *I didn't remember them bringing this here*, he thought and noticed the front tire was flat.

"You used to ride it a lot," Liam's father said. His head had appeared from the hatch.

"That was when we lived in Grand Rapids," Liam said.

"Your mom was always worried about where you and Matthew had gone."

They had lived in the countryside where numerous gravel roads had gone here and there in the forest and around the lake. Discovering where they led had provided endless adventures for the two young boys. *I wonder where Matthew is now*, Liam thought as he put the bike down.

Their freshman year in high school had just finished when Matthew's family had moved from Grand Rapids. The whole move had been a big mystery. Matthew's mother had told Liam that Matthew had become ill and couldn't be visited. A week later, the entire family had disappeared, and nobody knew where they had gone.

The whole summer, Liam had waited for Matthew to contact him. In the autumn, his sophomore year had begun, but Matthew wasn't there, and Liam still didn't know what had happened to him. The next summer, his family moved to Fairmont, and Liam had met Alex. Gradually, he'd thought of Matthew less and less.

"The boxes over there contain your old stuff," Liam's father said, pointing with his hand. "You could start with them. Keep whatever you want and throw the rest away."

"But those boxes are heavy," Liam protested.

"Pity that Alex can't help you," Mr. Green said. "I'm sure you'll be fine. Your mother and I are going to the grocery store in the meantime."

Liam sighed. He would have enjoyed his two-week vacation if his parents hadn't ordered a waste pick-up service. The men from the firm had delivered a huge trash container to their front yard that morning. Carrying the heavy stuff down a ladder wasn't precisely what Liam enjoyed. *Indeed, it's a pity that my muscular jock isn't here to help me.*

The first box contained books his mom had read him when Liam was a small baby. He could remember many of them, but as he browsed the stories, he found they weren't as exciting as they had been then. Liam dragged the heavy box to the hatch and wondered how to get it down. Eventually, he managed it, but his t-shirt was sweaty and his arms were hurting.

After the box was in the container, Liam climbed the ladder back to the attic. He was about to open the second box when he saw some something interesting on the wooden shelf. He had forgotten it, but there it was in the original package: his slot car racing set. Carefully, he pulled the box from the shelf.

I wonder if it still works, Liam thought as he held the box in his hands. He put it down on the floor and opened it. As soon as he saw the blue and red cars, he remembered the buzzing sound of the engines and the smell of electricity. *Matthew always wanted to drive the red car.*

When he was nine or ten, his parents gave him the racing set as a Christmas present. He and Matthew had sat on the floor of his bedroom for several days racing against each other. Matthew had won most of the time, but Liam hadn't minded. Besides, now and then, Matthew had let him cross the finish line first.

Liam resisted the temptation to put the pieces together and make a test run. Instead, he put the package back on the shelf and continued going through the cardboard boxes. The second contained his old toys, and luckily it wasn't as heavy as the first one. The third one was again full of books, and Liam seriously considered taking a shower after he had finally managed to carry it to the trash container.

Alex is so lucky he avoided this, Liam thought as he shook his hurting arms. He took a soda pop from the fridge and sat on the living room sofa. He turned on the television and watched cartoons for a while. When the episode ended, he returned to the attic to continue the cleaning project.

The fourth cardboard box had Liam's old clothes inside it. Given how small they looked, he had probably worn those when he was four or five. *Why did they save these clothes? Are they planning to have a baby?* Liam asked himself, but he was pretty sure if that were the case, his parents would have told him. Besides, his mother would soon turn fifty, which was pretty old to get pregnant.

Liam heard the doorbell ring. He put the clothes back in the box and climbed the ladder down to answer the door. He felt hungry and was happy his parents had returned from the grocery store. Hoping that Mom was making something good for lunch, he opened the door, but it wasn't his parents. A skinny young man around his age was standing on the porch.

"Hi, Liam," the guy said. "It's been a while."

"Matthew," Liam said. His friend looked different, but he would recognize that voice anytime. "Is it really you?"

Chapter 2

The tall, brawny athlete stood on the starting block ready to jump into the water. His wet blond hair was slicked back from his face, and his eyes were focused. His strong pecs tensed when he first raised his arms and then crouched, taking hold of the block with his hands.

"Raise your hips higher," Alex said.

Roy took a better position on the block. Alex walked around him and checked the placement of his arms and legs. He wanted to fix the angle of Roy's right foot a bit, but he didn't want to touch the badass jock. He took a couple of steps back and asked Roy to take the "take your mark" position.

"You need to pull back more," Alex instructed.

Roy stood up and glared at Alex. "Yeah, so you get a better view of my ass," he hissed and stepped off the block.

"What's your problem?" Alex asked.

"I want to talk to Coach Hanson and change to the other group," Roy said.

"Not gonna happen," Alex said as he turned to look at the rest of the group. "Who wants to try next?"

"Nobody," Roy said and crossed his arms.

He was wrong. Brandon, a small, dark-haired boy who had his goggles on his forearm, approached the starting block carefully. His face held a hint of hesitation, and he looked at Alex with his big brown eyes. Alex nodded and gestured for him to step up on the block.

"Okay. Let's start with the ready position," Alex said.

Brandon laughed nervously. "I'm not very good at this," he said quietly.

"Don't worry. We're here to practice," Alex said and glanced at Roy.

Alex moved Brandon's hands so there was a straight line from his shoulders to his hands. Then he showed him how to take a grip on the block and leave his thumbs on the front. Finally, he adjusted Brandon's legs to the right places on the block and pushed him gently on his lower back to set his body to the correct position.

"That's it. Very good. Now, relax your neck," Alex said and touched the muscles at the back of Brandon's neck.

Brandon breathed calmly and stared at the water in the pool. Somehow, it reminded Alex of his own first time practicing the start. Coach Hanson had fixed his hands and feet countless times; finally, finding the optimal became routine.

"Okay, take your mark," Alex said.

Brandon lowered his body too much. He was almost sitting on the block. Alex took hold of his hips and raised the boy so his back formed a nice coil. Then he moved a few steps farther to better see how Brandon looked on the block.

"There we go. That's perfect," he said.

"Cool. It wasn't that hard," Brandon said and stepped down from the block. He had a small smile on his face now.

"Okay. Who's next?" Alex asked.

"Let's stop this nonsense. You had your chance to grope us. We need a proper coach here," Roy shouted.

The blood in Alex's veins began to boil again. The boy seemed to know which buttons to push to get on his nerves, but Alex was determined not to give up. He looked at the rest of the group and nodded toward the block. Luckily, one of the older boys, Luke, volunteered quickly.

I think it's best I ignore Roy completely, Alex thought and turned Luke's feet a bit so his toes were pointing directly ahead before he asked him to take his mark. When he did, Luke pulled back a bit too much, the same way Brandon had done.

"Everyone, please come here and take a look," Alex said and waited until everybody, except Roy, had gathered around him. "If you pull yourself down like this, you'll lose the hamstring at the start."

"What's that?" one of the younger swimmers asked.

"It's the muscle here," Alex said and pointed to the back of Luke's thigh.

Alex explained the importance of the hamstring for an explosive start. He also promised to teach the swimmers some exercises to strengthen and stretch the muscle in the afternoon session. He had learned them from Tyler, who had been on the Eastwood swim team before Sam had killed him. Alex forced his thoughts quickly away from Sam and that dreadful day.

"Okay, let's fix this position," Alex said and put his hands on Luke's hips.

"Be careful, Luke. He's going to rape you," Roy shouted. Immediately, Alex let go of Luke.

Luke sighed. "Let's just ignore him."

Carefully, Alex took hold of Luke and raised his pelvis. The boy cooperated, and he didn't even seem to mind when Alex touched his lower back to push him down a little bit to get the position correct.

I'm making this a bigger thing than it really is. Coach Hanson fixed our starting positions all the time, Alex thought and tried to relax.

After everybody had practiced the start a few times, they dived into the pool and began swimming. Alex followed their performance in the adjacent lane and gave instructions on how to improve their swimming technique. Now and then, he took the opportunity to swim back and forth in the pool, which he hadn't done for several months. He was just swimming back from the other edge when Coach Hanson came to the pool.

"Just like old times," Coach Hanson said, watching his former student swim.

"I didn't realize how much I missed this," Alex said.

Coach Hanson noticed Roy, who was sitting on the bench. "Roy! Why aren't you practicing?" he shouted. The smile had disappeared from his face.

Roy stood up. "Um, sir," he said and rubbed his hands together.

"This isn't a vacation. We came here to practice," the coach said. "If you're not interested, you can take your lazy ass home."

Alex saw the scared expression on Roy's face. "His leg was hurting, so I asked him to rest a bit," he said.

Coach Hanson glanced at Alex, who tried to look as sincere as possible. He squinted his other eye—Alex knew what that meant—but Coach Hanson gave an approving grunt. Roy's leg experienced a miracle healing, though, and the boy was in the pool in the blink of an eye.

"Are you having problems with him?" Coach Hanson asked Alex.

"No. Everything is okay."

"Let me know if you need help with the kid. I'm pretty sure he lied about the hurting leg."

I'm pretty sure it was a lie, too, Alex thought and watched as the coach walked back to the main building. From the little he had seen, Alex believed Roy was a talented swimmer. His behavior implied his academic achievements might not be at the same level, and an athletic scholarship could be his only chance of getting into a decent college.

After fifteen minutes of swimming freestyle, Alex set the group to practice the butterfly stroke. Soon, he took Brandon to the other lane since the boy clearly needed some tutoring to perfect his technique. Patiently, Alex showed Brandon how to keep his elbows high and point his fingers toward the bottom of the pool. Brandon listened carefully and mimicked Alex as well as he could.

"Was that better?" Brandon asked after he had swum the lane back and forth.

"Much better," Alex said. The smile on Brandon's face made him feel satisfied. *Maybe I'm not a bad coach after all.*

Alex let Brandon join the others and checked how they were doing. Coach Hanson had done a great job with the kids, which didn't surprise Alex, and their swimming looked good. When Roy approached the end of the lane, Alex gestured for Roy to join him in the adjacent lane. The jock dived under the line marker and removed his goggles.

"I just want to give you a small tip," Alex said.

Roy gave him a suspicious look.

"When you pull, aim to keep your hands inside your body line," Alex said.

"Okay," Roy said slowly before pausing. "Is that all?"

Alex nodded. "Other than that, your strokes look great," he said.

They were both up to their necks in the water, holding on to the line marker. For many awkward seconds, they just stared at each other; neither of them said anything. Finally, Roy moved under the line marker back to the lane where the others were swimming.

"Thanks for the hint, I guess," he said, looking away from Alex. "And for the hurting leg," he added before he pushed with his legs from the edge of the pool and continued practice.

You're welcome, Alex thought, and a small smile appeared on his face.

"Hit the showers!" Coach Hanson's familiar voice echoed between the buildings. The boys came out of the water and rushed in. Alex lingered in the pool, enjoying what was left of the sun before it would set behind the mountains on the horizon. Practicing in an outdoor pool had its benefits.

"So, how do you like it?" Coach Hanson asked when Alex climbed the stairs out of the pool.

"It's great. Didn't have much time to get tan at Eastwood," Alex said.

"I meant coaching the kids. From what I've seen so far, you act like a pro."

"Learned from the best."

Alex grinned at the coach, who patted him on his shoulder. After a rough start, it felt good to get some recognition. Alex was especially pleased that Roy behaved during the theory class Alex taught after lunch. Also, when they returned to the pool, the boys had put their speedos on without additional hassle.

Maybe being open and honest was the best choice, Alex thought as he looked back at his time on the swim team. He had done his best to hide in the closet, and he had hurt his sweet boyfriend big time in the process. Luckily, those years were behind them.

"Thanks for giving me this job," Alex said when they were walking toward the main building.

"It's not me you should thank," the coach said, but then changed the topic quickly. "I've some business in the city. Could you take care of the kids and make sure they get supper and go to bed?"

Alex nodded, but his thoughts shifted to Roy and his friend. *If the coach is not here, will the boys follow my instructions?*

"Thanks, Alex. I knew I could trust you," Coach Hanson said.

They went into the building. Coach Hanson walked through the corridor and out of the door that led to the parking lot. Alex entered the locker room and took his towel before heading to the showers. Most of the boys were still there, washing their hair or just relaxing under the warm water. Alex looked around and saw Roy taking a shower in the corner. The only free showerhead was next to him.

Just my luck, Alex thought as he approached the empty slot. Now wasn't the best time to turn back, or he would lose what little was left of his authority.

Alex began showering, trying to ignore Roy as much as he could. Oddly, Roy didn't pay him any attention either. On the contrary, he had his back turned halfway toward Alex. Soon, Alex learned the reason. Despite his effort to cover it with his hand, Alex noticed that Roy's penis had grown. It wasn't fully erect but enough to make any teenage boy embarrassed.

Shit, I shouldn't be looking at it, Alex thought. When he raised his gaze, their eyes met. Under different circumstances, Alex would have laughed at the expression on Roy's face. While his cheeks and neck were red, his eyes communicated a combination of anger and annoyance. Without saying a word, Alex turned his face away and continued rubbing soap on his body.

When Alex returned to the locker room, Roy's friend was still there. He glared at Alex, who decided not to pay any attention to him. Instead, he dried his hair with the towel and began putting his clothes on.

"Supper will be served in the cafeteria in twenty minutes," Alex said to the boys in the locker room. "I'll give you your room keys after supper. Two people per room."

"Good luck to the one who sleeps with that homo," Roy's friend Kevin said, making sure everyone heard the comment.

"Thanks for the offer, but I have a boyfriend to sleep with," Alex said.

"Boyfriend," Kevin laughed. "Boys don't date each other."

Alex decided it was useless to continue the argument, so he took his bag and left the locker room. Roy had finished showering and almost walked into him in the corridor. Alex felt the urge to say something, but nothing came to mind. Also, Roy was avoiding his gaze as he rushed to the locker room.

When Alex reached the entrance hall, Luke approached him.

"I heard you study at Eastwood," Luke said. "Did you get a scholarship?"

"Um, yes … kind of," Alex said, "but I'm not on the swim team."

"Oh, cool. You do some other sport, too," Luke said. "What is it?"

Alex looked down and rubbed the back of his neck. "A charity organization pays my tuition. I'm not on any varsity team."

For some reason, Alex found it uncomfortable to tell Luke that the American Rainbow Association paid for his studies. He had gotten the scholarship at the last possible moment, thanks to Tyler, after his mother had died and his father had declined to fund his education.

Making the varsity team had been Alex's dream for as long as he could remember. It had been something his father had wanted, too. Not qualifying for the team had been the first step toward creating a gap between father and son. Alex's relationship with Liam had been the last nail, hit far too deep, in the coffin.

"You really should swim," Luke said. "Everyone says you're the best swimmer there has ever been at Fairmont High."

Alex smiled at Luke's enthusiasm. "You should see the Eddington Eagles swimming. Those guys are fast."

"They're good, but I want to join the Stanford Cardinals," Luke said.

"Oh…."

"I like the California weather."

39

Luke grinned at Alex and poked his arm. Alex watched him walking toward his friends, who were waiting for supper, and wondered if the boy seriously planned to apply to one of the most prestigious universities in the country. Luke did seem like a smart guy, so maybe he was serious.

The whole group, Alex and twenty high school boys, ate supper at the cafeteria. There were sandwiches and a big bowl of fruit served with water and orange juice. After everybody had finished, Alex gave the boys the keys to their cottages.

"You have some free time now, but be in your rooms by ten," Alex said to the boys. "Breakfast is tomorrow at six-thirty."

"Where's the coach?" one of the boys asked.

"Um, he had some business in town, but he should be here soon," Alex said.

"Cool! Nobody is watching us," Kevin said to Roy. The boys exchanged a high-five and walked out.

Alex wished Coach Hanson would return soon. Feeling nervous, he took his bag and began walking toward his cottage. Luckily, he didn't have to share it with anyone. Once he got into his room, he dropped his bag on one of the two beds and sat on the other.

I should call Liam and see how he's doing, Alex decided. The thought of hearing his boyfriend's soft voice made him smile. *My baby has been cleaning the house all day. He must be exhausted.*

The phone rang a couple times before it went to Liam's voicemail. Alex put the phone back in his pocket, assuming his boyfriend must be having supper with his parents and that Liam would call him back later. He always did, and probably it wouldn't take long before his phone started ringing.

Alex made sure the door was locked before he took off his jeans and lay down on the bed. He wanted to be prepared when Liam called. With some good luck, Liam would be alone, and they could have phone sex. Alex missed his boyfriend already; the most visible evidence was the massive tent in his boxers.

While waiting for the call, Alex kept rubbing his erection. The call never came, but Alex did.

An hour later, he left his room to make sure the boys were in their cottages. Coach Hanson hadn't arrived yet, which worried Alex. Luckily, the swim center looked quiet. Alex walked around the lodging area, but he couldn't see anyone, and there was no light coming from the cottages. The old storage was empty, and Alex even made sure nobody was hiding behind it.

It looks like they were too tired after practice, Alex thought, amused.

Just when he was returning to his cottage, he heard some voices behind the corner of the main building. Using his phone as a flashlight, he walked toward the noise but saw nobody.

"Anybody here?" Alex shouted.

"There's no one in here," somebody answered. It was followed by a burst of laughter.

Roy and Kevin, who had been hiding behind the porch railing, stood up. Both of them had a cigarette in their hands. In the dim light of the porch lamp, neither of them looked remorseful that Alex had found them. Kevin in particular had a big grin on his face.

"You should go to your room," Alex said. "It's past ten already."

"You go to your room and jerk off," Kevin said.

"Put out the cigarettes and go," Alex said. "Now!"

Neither of them showed any sign of obeying Alex. Instead, they continued smoking and chatting with each other like Alex wasn't there.

"You're just gonna stand there the whole night?" Roy said when Alex hesitated, unsure what to do.

"That homo probably gets a boner from watching us," Kevin said.

The blood in Alex's veins was boiling again. "Ask your friend who gets a boner," he snapped. As soon as he had said it, he noticed Roy glaring at him, his eyes flashing with anger.

Before anybody could say or do anything, they heard a car approaching the swim center. Roy and Kevin rushed to their cottage and closed the door before Coach Hanson's black BMW pulled into the parking area. Alex walked in the shadows back to his cottage and closed the door silently. He wasn't in the mood to explain to the coach what had just happened.

Chapter 3

Liam stared at his friend, still not sure if he should believe his eyes. Matthew had the same brown hair, just longer than when Liam had seen him the previous time. His face was slimmer, and his clothes looked oddly loose. Liam had to admit that Matthew was quite cute—and, more importantly, the smile in his eyes hadn't disappeared.

"How did you know I was here?" Liam asked.

"I didn't," Matthew said. "I found out your parents live here and thought they would know where you were."

"Where have you been all these years?" Liam asked the question that was burning in his mind.

"It's a long story. Can I come in?"

"Of course!"

Matthew had hardly passed the doorstep when Liam wrapped his arms around him and hugged him tightly. Matthew smiled shortly and finally patted Liam on his back a couple times. They let go of each other, and after an awkward moment of silence, Liam led his friend to the living room.

I can't believe he's here, Liam thought. Matthew scanned the furniture, the paintings on the walls, and the view to the backyard garden but said nothing. He carried a black bag with a red star logo on his shoulder. Liam remembered him having it when they were freshmen in high school.

"You graduated a year ago," Matthew said when he saw a photo of Liam on the bookcase.

"I'm studying history at Eastwood now," Liam said.

Matthew took the photo in his hand and studied it. Liam's mother had taken it of him and Alex on their graduation day. They were smiling and had their arms on each other's shoulders. When Matthew put the photo back on the shelf, Liam noticed he had been holding his breath.

"Are you in college?" Liam asked.

"Not right now," Matthew said and smiled at Liam. "I took a year off. I guess I don't know what I want to do yet."

"Probably a good idea to work and save some money before you start college then."

Liam desperately wanted to know everything that had happened to his best friend, and his mind was full of questions. The most burning topic was, of course, where and why Matthew and his family had moved, and why Matthew hadn't contacted him before now. Instead of overwhelming his friend with millions of questions, Liam decided to wait until Matthew was ready to tell him.

"I was cleaning the attic," Liam said. "Come on. There's something I want to show you."

Matthew followed Liam to the ladder, and they climbed up. When they crouched in the darkness of the attic to take a closer look at Liam's old bicycle, Liam felt like they were again in the Grand Rapids, Minnesota of his childhood. He and his best friend, together forever.

"I remember that bike," Matthew said. "It was your birthday present, wasn't it?"

I wanted it because you had such a cool bike, Liam thought. "Yeah, I think I was ten," he said.

"We rode all the way to the abandoned cabin."

"And then my front tire went flat, and we had to walk back."

It had been an awfully long trip back home, at least for two ten-year-old boys. They had made it barely half a mile before Liam had begun complaining about how tired he was. Finally, Matthew had taken both of the bikes and walked them to Liam's house, where his father had fixed the tire.

They opened one of the boxes Liam was supposed to carry to the trash container. On top, there was the Carcassonne game in a blue cardboard box. Liam picked up the game and looked at Matthew, who had a shy smile on his face.

"Sure, let's play," Matthew said. He looked at Liam like he was about to say something but turned his head away before any words came out.

Liam carried the game downstairs and set it on the kitchen table. Matthew helped him shuffle the terrain tiles and pick seven wooden meeples for each of them. He gave Liam the green meeples, according to his last name, and took the yellow ones himself. That was how they had always played in the school library or at home.

Nice to have you back, but where on earth have you been? Liam wondered as he studied his friend, who was trying to decide where to place his first tile.

They had set a couple dozen tiles on the table when the front door opened and Liam's mother walked into the kitchen with two huge shopping bags. Her husband followed him with another two bags. They looked surprised when they saw Liam sitting there with a strange boy.

"Oh, I didn't know you had a friend here," she said.

"Hi, Mrs. Green," Matthew said and nodded to Liam's father.

"Oh my god! Is it really you, Matthew?" she said, raising her voice an octave.

She left the shopping bags on the floor and rushed to hug the poor boy, who had barely managed to stand. Liam watched, amused at how his mother seemed unwilling to let go of his friend. Finally, she took a couple of steps back before she began shooting Matthew with a pattern of questions.

"Where do you live? Where did you move?" she said.

"Um, we moved to Russellville, Alabama," Matthew said, not making eye contact with any of them.

"I remember your mother saying her sister lives there."

Matthew was silent for a moment. Then he raised his gaze and said, "That's why we moved. She was ill and died soon after we got there."

"Oh, I'm so sorry to hear that," she said.

Liam stood still and waited for someone to say something. When nobody did, he opened his mouth and asked the question that had been bothering him since the end of his freshman year in high school. "Why didn't you tell me you were moving? And why didn't you call me?"

"I was so mad at my parents because they forced me to move," he said and looked Liam directly in the eye as he swallowed. "When we got there, I thought it didn't matter anymore because I was so far away from you."

Liam didn't know what to say. He just stared at his friend, trying to understand what he had heard.

"Can you forgive me?" Matthew said softly.

For the second time that morning, Liam hugged Matthew. "Of course. You're my best friend," he said and felt Matthew's hands pressing his back. "I'm so happy you're here."

Liam and Matthew helped prepare lunch, and soon the four of them were sitting at the kitchen table. The boys had moved their game to the living room, and Liam's mother had filled the table with half a dozen bowls and platters. She seemed pleased the boys were eating eagerly, especially Matthew.

"Have you already called Alex and told him Matthew's here?" she asked Liam.

Liam looked at his parents. His eyes were big, and he shook his head quickly. "No," he said and focused back on the food on his plate.

"Who's Alex?" Matthew asked.

"Um, he's a high school friend," Liam said. "He'll come over on Friday."

Liam's mother was about to say something when her husband touched her hand. They glanced at each other. After seeing the meaningful look on his face, she shrugged and began reminiscing about the time they lived in Minnesota when the boys were small. There were plenty of good stories before she remembered the blue sneakers.

"Liam always wanted to have clothes like yours," she said to Matthew. "I especially remember those shoes. We had to drive nearly two hundred miles to Minneapolis to find the right ones."

Matthew laughed and punched Liam's shoulder playfully. Liam blushed and hoped his mother would stop embarrassing him. Luckily, his father changed the subject.

"By the way, how did you get here? I didn't see a car parked outside," he asked.

"I took a bus," Matthew said.

"Oh, that must have been a long journey."

"Nearly twenty hours."

"Wow! And you didn't even know that I was here," Liam said, surprised.

"Um… I guess I was really lucky," Matthew said, looking at his plate.

Indeed, Liam thought and noticed his parents glancing at each other. Matthew's long trip sounded crazy, but he was happy his friend had done it.

After lunch, Liam's mother offered Matthew the opportunity to take a shower, which he gladly accepted. It must have been tough to sit for so many hours on a bus. Liam caught a glimpse of Matthew walking to the bathroom with only a towel wrapped around his waist. *He's definitely leaner than before,* he thought and couldn't help liking what he saw.

"I assume you haven't told him about you and Alex," Liam's father said after they heard water coming from the shower.

"Do you remember how religious his parents were?" Liam said.

"If you want to be friends again, you need to tell him."

"I know, but I don't want to do it yet. I just got him back."

Liam was thankful his parents hadn't taken him to church on Sundays. He knew how much Alex had suffered from a mother who considered homosexuality the worst of sins. *What if Matthew and his family thought the same?* Liam pondered. He wasn't ashamed of who he was. If needed, he would come out to the entire Eastwood University, but suddenly, telling Matthew felt difficult.

Matthew returned from the bathroom and got dressed in Liam's bedroom. Liam's mother stopped him as soon as he entered the kitchen.

"Oh, honey. You've spent hours on the bus. Let me wash that shirt for you. Liam will loan you a clean one," she said and looked at her son.

"Thanks, but this will do fine," Matthew said as he studied the front of his shirt.

"Let's go. You know, it's better to do as she says," Liam said and led Matthew back to his room.

Liam's wardrobe was full of his old clothes, which he hadn't taken with him to Eastwood. There was far too little storage space in their small but cozy dorm room, even after Alex had allowed him to use an additional shelf in his closet. Liam chose the biggest shirt he could find since Matthew was a bit taller than him.

"Thanks," Matthew said as he began taking off his shirt.

"What's that?" Liam asked when he saw a bruise and a scratch on Matthew's side.

"Oh, it's nothing. I must've hit it somewhere."

Matthew put on Liam's shirt. It was a bit tight, but Liam thought that it emphasized Matthew's pecs and lean body nicely. If it had been Alex, he wouldn't have been able to resist the temptation to run his fingers down his chest. Since it wasn't, he just stared at his good-looking friend. Soon, his mother came to pick up Matthew's old shirt and put it in the washing machine.

The boys went to the living room to continue their game. Liam won the first, Matthew the second and third. Liam followed how Matthew set his meeples on the terrain tiles, and his mind traveled back in years to the small school library in Grand Rapids. They had sometimes sat there for hours just playing.

Liam's mother came into the living room and saw them playing. "Matthew, would you like to stay the night here?"

"Um, I have no other plans, so if it's not too much trouble for you," he said tentatively.

"Not at all," she said. "I'll get some extra pillows and blankets and make you a bed in the guest room."

"Oh, that's not necessary. There are two beds already made in Liam's room. I can sleep there," Matthew said. "If that's okay with you?" he added and turned to look at Liam.

"Um, sure," Liam said, though he suddenly wasn't so sure that was a good idea.

Liam felt his phone ringing in his pocket. It was Alex. He wanted to answer, but at the same time, he didn't want to tell Matthew he had a boyfriend. He declined the call.

"Who was it?" his mom asked.

"Nobody. Just a guy from the university," Liam said and put the phone back in his pocket.

Liam woke up early the following morning. He heard quiet breathing coming from the adjacent bed and was about to hug the sleeping boy before he realized it wasn't Alex. Instead, he sat up. Soon, Matthew turned around and opened his eyes.

"Morning, sunshine," Matthew said, smiling.

Liam held the blanket tightly on his lap. "Did you sleep well?" he asked.

"Better than I have in a long time."

Matthew's bed hair looked funny, and it reminded Liam of the sleepovers they used to have, mostly in his bedroom. Matthew had usually awakened him by tickling his neck or feet. On rainy days, the boys had sat on the floor playing board games. Otherwise, they had taken their bikes and ridden to the lake or along the gravel roads in the forest as soon as they had eaten breakfast.

The day Liam realized the old red truck he had seen from the kitchen window had been transporting the Evans' furniture and other belongings away from their neighborhood was one of the saddest in his life. He had spent a lonely summer and sophomore year at high school before his family had moved, too. And now both of them were in his bedroom in Fairmont.

"I still can't believe you're here," Liam said.

Matthew looked away. "I'm so sorry I didn't contact you," he said.

"How was your high school in Russellville?"

"Um, normal, I guess."

Matthew's face grew severe. He took the shirt Liam had loaned him and put it on. It was a warm summer day, and he had been sleeping without it. Then he stood up from the bed and with his back toward Liam, he pulled on his shorts. When he sat on the chair and turned to look at Liam again, the familiar smile had returned to his eyes.

"How was high school here?" Matthew asked. "At least you made some friends," he added.

"How do you know?"

"I saw the other boy in the photo."

"Ah, yeah. That's Alex."

They heard a knock on the door, followed by an announcement from Liam's mother that breakfast was ready. Liam adjusted the crotch of his boxer briefs quickly before he grabbed his shorts from the floor and put them on, still hiding under the blanket. Then both of them followed the smell of freshly fried bacon to the kitchen.

Liam was amazed when he saw how much food Matthew collected on his plate. *How on earth can he be so slim if he eats that much?* Liam chose his favorite: pancakes and strawberry jam. He was sure his mom had made them because he had come home.

"Do you have a girlfriend at Eastwood?" Matthew asked out of the blue when Liam was starting to eat his second pancake.

"Um, I'm dating someone," Liam said, not looking Matthew in the eyes.

"Okay, cool," Matthew said casually and continued eating.

Liam was grateful Matthew didn't want to know more about his *girlfriend*. He looked at his parents, expecting to see their judgmental gazes. They weren't judging him, though, but both gave him a small nod, so subtle that Matthew didn't notice their silent communication.

After they had eaten, Matthew excused himself to go to the bathroom, and Liam helped his mother clean the table. His father fetched a roll of black plastic bags. He planned to throw away all the unnecessary items in the garage.

"How disappointed would you be if I didn't help you clean the house today?" Liam asked tentatively. "I would like to show Matthew around Fairmont."

His parents looked at each other. "We understand," his father said.

"Thanks!" Liam said, and a wide smile grew on his face. "And thanks for not telling Matthew about Alex."

"It's not our job to tell him," his father said and patted Liam on his shoulder.

"Take my car and have fun," his mother added.

The boys took quick showers—exceptionally quick for Liam, who loved to stay under the steaming hot water—and climbed into the car. Since Alex was always sitting behind the wheel when they went somewhere, Liam hadn't driven a car for several months. Carefully, he turned onto the road and began driving toward his old high school.

"You lived here two years?" Matthew said.

"I started my junior year here," Liam said.

"Why did you move?"

Because my parents suspected that I was gay and they thought that it would be easier for me here than without any friends in that small town in Minnesota, Liam thought. "Dad got a job here," he said.

"Is he still selling those medical instruments?" Matthew asked.

"Yes. He has many clients here, but he travels to other states, too," Liam said. "What do your parents do?"

"Um, my mom … she's still a nurse," Matthew said.

"And your father?"

"He has his own bookkeeping firm."

Liam turned left at the traffic light, and the massive red brick building, Fairmont High School loomed in front of them on top of a small hill. Next to it were the baseball stadium and the swim hall. Matthew looked at the buildings.

"I assume you didn't become a jock when you moved here," Matthew said with a grin.

Liam laughed. "Nope. The same nerd as in Grand Rapids."

"Your friend in the photo looks more athletic."

Liam froze. It was already the second time Matthew had referred to Alex. "Alex was on the swim team," he said.

Suddenly, a big black SUV came from the right and turned in front of them. Liam noticed it at the last moment and hit the brake. The tires of his mother's car squealed and left black marks on the asphalt. But, what was most important, they avoided the collision.

"Careful, dude," Matthew said.

Liam's heart was beating fast. "Shit. I didn't see it coming."

"Yeah. You were so eager to show me your old school," Matthew said and poked Liam on his shoulder.

They parked the car in the empty parking lot and walked toward the main building. It reminded him of those times when he had walked to his old high school in Grand Rapids with Matthew, but even more, he thought of Alex, who had driven him to the high school many times. They had parked Alex's Mustang in the same parking area and walked the same path. The only difference was there had been other students. Now, he and Matthew were the only ones in the schoolyard.

"How long did you plan to stay in Fairmont?" Liam asked.

"I don't know. I guess I'll need to leave today."

"Today? Why?"

"Your parents are cleaning the house. I don't want to disturb them more."

Liam thought of what Matthew had said. If Matthew left now, he had no idea when he would see his friend next. He and Alex would soon return to Eddington, and he hadn't even had a chance to tell Matthew about Alex. They walked through the gate, and neither of them said anything. Suddenly, Liam came up with an idea.

"How about if we go camping for a couple of days before you leave?" he said.

"Like we did every summer," Matthew said, excitement in his voice.

"I know a nice national park here," Liam said. "I went there a couple years ago with my … parents."

"Okay, sounds like a plan. Let's go."

After Liam had shown Matthew around Fairmont High School, they drove to the mall where Liam's mother worked. It still looked the same. Some shops had closed and new ones had opened, but Liam recognized most of the places there—even the restaurant where he had almost had a date with Alex until Rick had spoiled it.

On their way back home, they passed by the big house where Alex had lived. Liam wanted to see it. Of course, he didn't mention anything to Matthew when he slowed down to take a closer look at the place. *It's sad the Wesleys don't live there anymore*, Liam thought. He couldn't say he especially liked Alex's parents after what they had done to Alex, but what had happened to Alex's father after his mother had died wasn't something he wished for anybody.

When they got back home, Liam suggested Matthew wait in his room. He wanted to talk to his parents alone. He watched them preparing lunch in the kitchen as he wondered how to formulate the question.

"Honey, I know that face," his mother said and stopped chopping the lettuce.

"Um, I would like to ask something," Liam said and scratched his left hand.

"Your father and I can clean the house, if that is worrying you," she said. "Besides, we're almost finished already."

"Would you mind if Matthew and I went camping for a couple days?"

"To Ebikon Park? I need the car, but I can drive you there after lunch."

A relaxed smile appeared on his face when Liam realized he could still spend a couple days with his friend before Matthew had to return to Russellville.

Leaving all the cleaning to his parents didn't feel right after he had promised to help them.

"Have you told Matthew about Alex yet?" she asked.

Liam shook his head. "But I will, soon," he said.

I should tell Alex, too.

Chapter 4

Matthew swallowed and looked around. Liam's bedroom had many items from his time in high school: books on the shelf, his senior-year schedule and diploma on the wall, and a set of color pens on the table next to the laptop, which looked brand new.

After checking one more time that nobody could see him, Matthew sealed the zip-lock bag he was holding in his hand and put it back in the side pocket of his backpack. Then he sneaked to the doorway and tried to listen to the discussion in the kitchen.

"Have you told Matthew about Alex already?"

He couldn't hear how Liam answered his mother, but it seemed his best friend was hiding something.

Don't worry, man. A lot has happened since we last met, Matthew thought and moved quickly to sit on the bed when he heard Liam coming.

"Mom promised to drive us to the park after lunch," Liam said, his eyes wide as he rushed to his wardrobe. "We can be there until Friday."

Matthew watched as Liam took a pile of shirts from the closet and chose which ones to pack. Next, he picked a couple pairs of shorts and hiking pants and began matching them with the colors of the shirts. It reminded Matthew of those times when he had been waiting in Liam's room for his friend to get dressed so they could walk to school together.

"I hope three nights is okay with you?" Liam said and turned to look at his friend.

"Um, sure," Matthew said. He raised his backpack from the bed. Despite the phone charger, it was more or less empty.

"Do you have enough clothes?" Liam asked.

"Not really," Matthew said and looked down. "I wasn't expecting a camping trip," he laughed.

"Don't worry. You can borrow mine."

Liam browsed the items at the back of the lowest shelf and handed Matthew some shirts, socks, and boxers. Matthew folded them and put them in his backpack while Liam went to check whether his father had hiking pants and boots his friend could borrow. In no time at all, they had gathered everything they would need during their short trip to the national park.

"How come you had so little stuff when you came here?" Liam asked.

"Huh? What do you mean?" Matthew said, pretending he hadn't understood the question.

"Well, you traveled hours on a bus, but you don't have any spare clothes," Liam said. "If I know your mother at all, she would've packed half your clothes for even a one-night trip."

Feeling his cheeks warming up, Matthew looked at Liam, who was smirking. That might have been true when they lived in Grand Rapids. Now things were more complicated.

"I managed to escape when she wasn't watching," Matthew said.

"You probably shouldn't have," Liam said.

You have no idea, Matthew thought but said nothing. The mention of his mother filled his head with feelings of hatred and disgust. He tried to force her out of his mind, but it was difficult. She had ruined everything, and that was something he would never forgive her for.

Matthew forced his thoughts to his friend. *He has moved on. University and everything.* Matthew was sad he hadn't been part of Liam's life during the past four years. Even now, when they were in the same room, Matthew felt he had lost something he could never get back. Nothing would turn the clock and take them back to the end of their freshman year in Grand Rapids.

"How is it studying at the university?" Matthew asked.

"I love it. People are much cooler than in high school," Liam said.

"You live there? You have roommates?"

"Um, just one. He is … he's a nice guy. Studies computer engineering."

"Wow. Must be an even bigger geek than you."

Seeing Liam smiling improved Matthew's mood. Maybe one day they could get back what they once had: two best friends joking and spending time together.

"Your high school friend, this Alex, where does he study?" Matthew asked, fishing for more information about this mysterious guy.

"Um, he's at Eastwood, too," Liam said.

What is it about him you haven't told me? Matthew pondered whether he should just ask it directly, but he was worried it would upset Liam now when they had found each other again. Then his phone began ringing and interrupted their discussion.

Shit, Maria. I have a pretty good idea why my dear sister is calling, Matthew thought. Without hesitation, he declined the call and switched off the phone.

"Who was it?" Liam asked, surprised.

"There was no caller ID," Matthew said. "Probably someone trying to sell something."

"Yeah. I hate those calls," Liam said.

Soon, Liam's mother called them for lunch, and they all gathered in the kitchen. After everybody had sat down, they began passing the bowls until everyone had filled their plates. Matthew placed a big chicken fillet on his plate and stared longingly at the rest of the fillets that were swimming in curry sauce.

"Please take more. You must be hungry," Liam's mother encouraged him.

Matthew didn't need to be told twice. "Thanks, ma'am," he said and took another fillet.

"She's always glad when someone likes her cooking," Liam's father whispered to Matthew.

"Only an idiot wouldn't like this," Matthew said, taking a bite of chicken.

"We're all so happy you came to visit us," Liam's mother said. She had a big smile on her face—it was evident from whom Liam had inherited his gestures—and she looked Matthew straight in the eyes.

Matthew nodded and smiled back. He had always secretly envied Liam for the warm atmosphere in their house. Apparently, that hadn't changed after they moved to Fairmont. He wished he would have gotten even the slightest piece of it.

She wouldn't welcome my visit here, Matthew thought, wishing he didn't need to care about his mother's opinion.

"So, do you work somewhere?" Mr. Green asked. "Liam told us you're not studying at the moment."

Matthew tried not to blush but failed. "Um, I clean tables in a local cafe," he said.

"Nothing wrong with that," Mr. Green said. "These times, it's good to have any job. You can earn some money before you continue your studies."

I guess so, Matthew thought and hoped Liam's father didn't want to know more about his job. He was so friendly and meant well, but the more they talked about his work shifts and the customers at the cafe, the more uncomfortable Matthew felt.

Soon, it'll be just the two of us in the forest, he thought and looked at Liam, who was spreading butter on his bread.

"I'm starting to work in a coffee shop, too, in a couple of weeks after we—after I return to Eddington," Liam said.

"What a coincidence," Mrs. Green said. "From what I remember, you always did everything together. Now you have even the same jobs."

Matthew forced a smile on his face and continued eating his food. Suddenly, he began laughing hysterically. Liam turned to look at his friend; his parents looked at each other. It took some time before Matthew could speak again.

"Oh, I'm so sorry," he said and tried to take a breath. "I just suddenly remembered the time when Liam was eating with us. I guess it was just after Christmas. We were still in middle school. He poured a full bowl of beetroot soup on his lap."

"I remember your mother's face," Liam said. "I was so worried I would never be welcome at your house again."

It wasn't because of the soup, Matthew thought, and the smile disappeared from his face. During the rest of lunch, he mostly listened to the Greens' discussion, trying to clean his plate. The chicken, no matter how delicious it was, had a hard time going down his throat.

When lunch was over, the boys took their backpacks, and Liam's mother drove them to Ebikon National Park. Liam talked to him most of the ride, but it wasn't until she stopped the car in front of the big map near the entrance that Matthew realized he hadn't been listening. He opened the door and rushed toward the bushes.

"I need to take a pee," he shouted, carrying his backpack on his right shoulder as he jogged away from the car. Too embarrassed to look back, he crouched behind a large rock and wished he had come up with a better excuse.

Matthew helped Liam set up the tent in a clearing they had found near the riverbank. After they had unfolded the tent, they connected the stakes to the flaps on each corner and pushed them into the soft ground. Then they put the tent poles together and raised the tent.

"This should hold," Matthew said after he had connected the rope that was holding the pole to the ground with a stake.

"Have you seen the last stake?" Liam asked, holding his rope in his hand.

"Let's cut a branch from those trees," Matthew said. "We can tie the rope to it."

"Damn. How could I be so stupid?" Liam cursed. "I forgot to pack a knife."

"Don't worry. You can borrow mine," Matthew said and took a pocket knife from the side pocket of his backpack. Effortlessly, he opened it and gave it to Liam.

"How on earth can a guy who doesn't even have spare boxers carry a knife?" Liam said, amused, and went to fetch a branch that he could use as a tent stake.

"You never know when you'll be invited to go camping!" Matthew shouted.

The last time he had needed the knife was just a few weeks ago, when a drug addict and his friends had tried to steal Matthew's money—not that he had much. He had used the knife to clear his way through the gang to escape the alley.

Being in the silent park was a welcomed change. Matthew watched how innocently Liam used the knife to carve a stake that would hold the tent pole. *That's so cute. Just like the old days*,

"That should work," Liam said and tied the rope to the stake. "Look how skillful I am."

"We would have been so screwed without the survival skills they teach at the university." Matthew had a big smirk on his face.

Liam handed the knife back. Instinctively, Matthew put it in his pocket. If anyone came to threaten their camping trip, he could use it to defend them. *Nobody hurts Liam on my watch*, he thought as he looked around. Despite the beautiful summer day, there were no other people in the area.

They sat on the riverbank and watched as the sun slowly set. It had taken them a couple of hours to walk there and set up the tent, so it was already late afternoon. Matthew moved closer to Liam; for a moment, he felt like they were small kids in Grand Rapids again.

"You haven't said much about what you want to study," Liam said.

Matthew looked at his friend and saw the same person who had always encouraged him to do his homework. *You won't get a good job if you don't do your homework*. Matthew laughed at Liam's words. Or probably they were his parents'. Either way, he had heard them many times.

"I need to tell you something," Matthew said. *He's gonna hate this so much.*

Liam waited for his friend to continue. "You can tell me anything," he encouraged.

Matthew sighed. "I didn't finish high school," he finally said in a quiet tone, looking away from Liam.

He had started his sophomore year in Alabama, but after months of meeting the hypocritical therapist in those ridiculous sessions, he had hated himself so much that he didn't want to see the other kids at school. He had managed to skip classes for three months before the principal called his parents.

"After Aunt Martha died, everything was so screwed up in our family," Matthew said.

"I'm so sorry. I didn't know you were so close to her," Liam said.

I don't give a shit about her, Matthew thought. His life had been nothing but hell ever since they had moved to her big house. The old maid had lived there most of her life and she lived there still with his parents.

"Have you thought about finishing school one day?" Liam asked.

"I guess I should."

"Just let me know if I can help you somehow."

They watched as the sun disappeared behind the horizon. Suddenly, Liam put his arm around Matthew's shoulder and patted him a couple of times before pulling it away. Matthew hadn't felt such compassion for years. His eyes became moist, and he had to blink them so Liam wouldn't notice.

It was getting dark, and they were in the middle of a forest. Still, for the first time since leaving Grand

Rapids, Matthew felt like he wasn't completely lost. The long bus trip to Fairmont had been worth it.

"Should we start a fire?" Liam said. "I'm starving already."

"Sounds like a good idea," Matthew said and stood up. "I'll go gather some wood."

Feeling his mood improve, Matthew fetched a flashlight from the tent and searched for small branches from the nearby forest. It didn't take long until he had enough so they could cook some supper. Liam had already taken a couple of food boxes from his backpack and was pouring water into a pot when Matthew returned with an armful of firewood.

They started the fire, and when the water began boiling, Liam added the pasta and some salt. Then he tried to open the canned meat his mother had bought them on their way to the park.

"Damn. I can't get this open," Liam said after several attempts to open the lid.

"Let me help," Matthew said and took the can. With one strong pull, it was open.

"And that's why Alex is the one who always cooks."

"Alex? Your friend from high school?"

"Um, yes. He's my … roommate at Eastwood."

Because of the darkness, it was hard for Matthew to see if Liam was blushing. They had known each other long enough that Matthew noticed there was something strange in Liam's behavior.

Why did he tell me only now that this mysterious Alex is his roommate? Matthew was not sure if he would like the answer. If his assumption was correct, he wouldn't like it at all.

Trying hard to hide his growing concerns, Matthew watched as Liam poured most of the water away and mixed the meat and some canned sauce with the pasta. He kept it on the fire a few more minutes to make sure it was warm and then split the contents onto two plates. He gave one to Matthew.

"Thanks. This is good," Matthew said when the silence had lasted too long.

"Yeah. For someone who lets his roommate take care of all the cooking," Liam said.

"Tell me about the city. Eddington," Matthew said to change the topic.

Liam started telling him about Eastwood University before he described the beautiful parks, the big office district full of international companies, and the huge shopping mall north of the city. It sounded nothing like Grand Rapids or Russellville.

I wish I could live in a place like that, Matthew thought. He had to admit that any change to his current living arrangement would be a major improvement.

The fresh air and long walk to the camping area had made them tired. After Liam had finished telling his friend about his new hometown, they decided to go to sleep. Liam began undressing in the tent, but Matthew crawled inside his sleeping bag before he took off his shirt and pants. Despite there being only gloomy light from the lantern, he didn't want Liam to see him in his boxers. Not before he knew the truth about Alex.

"Good night," Liam said after they were all set. He reached for the lantern and switched it off.

Should I just ask him? Matthew pondered in the darkness. The voice inside his head kept telling him to do it. The elephant in the tent was getting bigger and bigger.

"Liam?" he whispered finally and heard his friend mutter something in response. "Are you gay?"

Chapter 5

Liam heard Matthew whispering his name. Next came the question, which made his body tense: "Are you gay?"

Should I just pretend I didn't hear him? Liam thought but realized that it would be stupid. Matthew would just ask it again.

"Why would you ask that?" he said to buy some time.

"Are you?" Matthew repeated the question.

Answering the question felt hard. *What if he doesn't accept my being gay?* he thought. The rest of their days in the national park would be awkward if Matthew avoided him. Not to mention sleeping in the same small tent.

Better than ever, Liam understood why it had been so difficult for Alex to date him openly in high school.

It wasn't just his parents. He was afraid he would lose his friends, too, he realized.

"Alex isn't just my roommate. He's also my boyfriend," Liam said finally, not wanting to lie to his friend.

Matthew didn't say anything, but Liam could hear in the darkness of the tent that he unzipped his sleeping bag. When Liam found his flashlight, he saw Matthew crawling out of the tent in his boxers, dragging his backpack with him.

"Please, don't go," Liam said. "Let's talk."

There was no reply.

When Liam got out of the tent, he scanned the surroundings with the flashlight. No matter where he pointed the light, he couldn't catch a glimpse of Matthew. He tried to call his friend with no success either.

Since he had no idea where Matthew had gone, Liam returned to the tent. He took his phone from his pocket and cursed when there was no signal. Also, the battery was almost drained, so he switched it off in case he needed it later.

I guess I can only wait until he comes back. If he comes, Liam thought and pondered whether it had been a mistake to tell Matthew. On the other hand, if they were supposed to be friends again, he would have found it out sooner or later anyway.

We were best friends for years. I assumed he would be more accepting, Liam thought bitterly and felt like he had lost his friend for the second time. Maybe Matthew wasn't worth his friendship. The more he thought about it, the more Liam wanted to get back to the university campus where everybody was so friendly and understanding.

Shit. Alex! I should have called him. Liam realized he had been so excited about Matthew and the camping trip that he hadn't let Alex know where he was. It was too late now, but Liam hoped Alex would call his parents since his phone could not be reached before Friday.

Liam had just fallen asleep when Matthew came back to the tent. Liam stood up, as much as he could in the small tent, and switched on the lantern.

"Um, how are you?" he asked.

Matthew laughed. "You're funny when you look so concerned," he said and put his backpack next to his sleeping bag.

"Of course I'm concerned," Liam said, raising his voice. "You left without saying a word."

"I'm so sorry," Matthew said with a wide grin on his face. "I had to think about it a bit."

"And are you okay with it? That I'm … gay."

"Of course. Come here and let me hug you."

Liam rolled his eyes but moved closer to Matthew, who wrapped his arms around him. It could have been a bit awkward, two friends on their knees dressed in nothing but boxers, but Liam didn't mind.

I'm so happy he doesn't care that I'm gay, he thought and squeezed Matthew harder against his bare chest.

Finally, they let go of each other. Matthew gave Liam puppy dog eyes.

"Can you forgive me for leaving so suddenly?" he said.

"How can I resist that face?" Liam replied.

Matthew laughed again. "Wanna go swimming?"

"Now? In the middle of the night? Let's sleep first."

"You're so rational and boring," Matthew said and poked Liam's chest. "Good night then," he added and crawled inside his sleeping bag.

Good night to you, too, Liam thought. The course of the events confused him. The sudden change of Matthew's behavior—no matter how welcome it was—concerned him. Then his thoughts shifted to Matthew's parents.

Maybe they have taught him that homosexuality is a sin. Or something even worse. Perhaps that explains his first reaction, Liam rationalized. He had never talked about the topic with them, but he was sure Mr. and Mrs. Evans represented the conservative side.

Coming from that perspective, the half-naked hug and crazy proposal to go swimming were kind of cute. Of course, Matthew wanted to show him that they were friends no matter what. That was how he had always been.

Then there was the hug. During their freshman year in high school, and even before that, Liam had developed feelings for Matthew. He had never told his friend, and after Matthew's family had moved away, he had gradually buried them somewhere deep in his soul—so deep they were never meant to pop up again.

We are friends, and that's it, Liam told himself but he couldn't help thinking of the boy who was sleeping next to him.

Liam walked along the riverbank. Farther down, where the river turned left, he saw the beach where he and Alex had been swimming on that beautiful summer day two years ago. The next morning, Liam's father had found them making out in the tent. Alex's reaction amused him now.

He thought they didn't know we were more than friends, Liam called the incident that had shocked his boyfriend.

It was still early morning and a bit chilly, but the cloudless sky anticipated a hot day. Liam awakened half an hour earlier and, after watching his sleeping friend for a while, crawled out of the tent carefully to avoid waking Matthew.

Liam started to prepare breakfast. He poured water into the pot to steep some tea. While waiting for the water to boil, he fried a couple eggs. When everything was ready, he put out the campfire and set four pieces of bread to toast on the pan that was still hot. Then he went to wake Matthew.

He opened the tent and pushed his head inside. "Good morning, sunshine," he said.

There was no reaction. Matthew kept breathing steadily, and his eyes remained closed. Liam crawled inside the tent and poked his friend to wake him up. Finally, Matthew cracked his eye and muttered something.

"Breakfast is ready," Liam said cheerfully. He opened the tent doors to let sunlight in.

"I'm not hungry," Matthew said and pulled the sleeping bag to cover his face.

Liam tugged the bag away from Matthew's face and was about to open the zipper when he realized how pale his friend was. "Are you okay? You look awful."

"I'm just not a morning person. Can I still sleep? Please."

"But I just made us breakfast."

Matthew took his backpack and followed Liam out of the tent. His face was white, and he was breathing heavily when he stood up in front of the tent. Watching his friend wearing nothing but boxers and the backpack, Liam would have found the situation hilarious if he hadn't been so concerned.

"Are you sure you're okay?" he asked again.

"Yeah, I guess."

"Let's have some tea and toast. I fried some eggs, too," Liam said proudly.

"Sorry but I don't feel like I can eat anything," Matthew said and knitted his brows. "I need to take a leak."

Liam watched as Matthew rushed to the nearby forest and disappeared behind the bushes. He waited a few minutes and, when he didn't see Matthew anywhere, he poured himself some tea and began eating the egg sandwiches. They were okay but not as good as the ones his mother made.

I hope he's not getting sick, Liam thought and checked what medicine he had with him. He found only band-aids and painkillers, which probably wouldn't help if it was something serious.

After fifteen minutes had passed, Liam started to be really worried. Matthew hadn't returned. *I need to go and find him*, Liam thought as he jogged toward the forest where Matthew had gone, shouting his name on the way.

"Don't worry, sweetheart. I'm here." Matthew appeared behind the trees. He was grinning, and his face had its normal color again.

"Damn you. I was worried sick," Liam said, looking unhappy. *And why is he calling me sweetheart?*

"I'm so sorry," Matthew said and made his best puppy face.

Liam sighed, but the smile was gradually coming back to his face. After all, Matthew seemed to be okay. And, as if the morning hadn't been odd enough, Matthew decided to hug him. After a moment of hesitation, Liam also wrapped his arms around his friend, and they stood there holding each other.

"I'm so sorry," Matthew repeated when they let go of each other. "I'm just not a morning person."

Liam nodded and looked at his friend, taking in first his eyes, then the scar on his stomach, and finally his gaze met with Matthew's boxers. *Is it just my imagination, or is the bulge getting bigger?* he thought and glanced away.

They walked back to the tent. Liam stole another glance at the front of Matthew's boxers but couldn't get confirmation of his observation. Then his curiosity made him feel guilty. *I'm sure Alex has been admiring other guys in the gym shower*, he tried to rationalize.

"Yum. This is good," Matthew said after tasting the sandwich Liam had made.

"It must be cold already," Liam said.

Matthew stuffed the rest of the toast in his mouth. "Could you please make me another?" he said after he had swallowed everything.

"Are you serious?"

"Please, please, please," Matthew said and stood to hug Liam.

"Okay, okay," Liam said to his friend, who approached him with his arms wide open.

Liam stoked the campfire again and waited until the pan was hot. Then he poured some oil in the pan, fried an egg, and heated some bread. Matthew watched him sitting on the ground leaning against his backpack. He was still dressed in nothing but his boxers.

"Have you been training at the gym or something?" Liam asked.

"Are you looking at my naked body?" Matthew said.

"Sorry," Liam said. He blushed and turned his head quickly away.

Matthew laughed at Liam's reaction. "I'm just kidding."

Getting back to where they had been four years ago was hard, which frustrated Liam. Disregarding that he was older and taller, Matthew still looked the same. He sounded the same, but there was something different, although Liam couldn't identify it. And it made it hard for him to reconnect with the best friend he had ever had.

Maybe I'm just trying too hard, he thought and decided to give them more time.

After Matthew had finished his breakfast, he suggested they go for a swim. Liam was about to get his swim trunks from the tent when Matthew stopped him. Speechless, Liam watched as Matthew pulled his boxers down and ran naked to the river until his bare butt was below the water.

"Are you coming?" Matthew shouted and splashed water with his hands.

"Um…." Liam hesitated.

"Hurry up! It's warm."

Reluctantly, Liam took off his t-shirt. It didn't help that Matthew was staring at him incessantly with a wider and wider grin on his face. Finally, Liam got the courage to pull down his shorts and boxer briefs. Feeling his cheeks burning, he approached the river, covering his crotch with both hands. As soon as the water was up to his knees, he crouched in the water and began swimming.

Matthew swam to him and took hold of his elbow. They were now standing in the water, which was almost up to their necks.

"Think about if someone came and found us here naked," Matthew said.

Liam looked around but couldn't see anybody. "Should we go and get dressed?" he said.

"Why are you such a mama's boy?" Matthew said and pushed Liam on his chest. "Besides, we just got here."

Although Liam had enjoyed playing with Alex in the water a few years earlier, Matthew's horseplay made him feel uncomfortable. More than anything, he regretted his decision to come swimming naked, especially since

Matthew was constantly trying to engage him in some wrestling match.

When Matthew swam a bit farther, Liam waded to the shore, ignoring his friend's repeated pleas to get back into the water. Under the cover of the tent, Liam dried himself and got dressed. When he emerged from the tent, Matthew was standing on the riverbank grinning.

What's wrong with him? He's been acting weird the whole morning, Liam thought but couldn't help staring at Matthew's naked body. Matthew noticed it but said nothing. Liam turned his head, hoping, in vain, that his interest in his friend's crotch hadn't been obvious.

"Could you please get dressed?" Liam said turning his back to his friend.

Liam heard Matthew laughing. Still, he obeyed the request because he was wearing a t-shirt and shorts when he poked Liam on his back a few moments later.

"Better now, Mr. Decency?" Matthew asked.

Liam gave a theatrical sigh, but soon a small smile appeared on his face. "You're weirder than I remember," he said.

"Is it a bad thing?"

Liam gave Matthew a meaningful look. Maybe it wasn't such a bad thing. Considering that one of his closest friends, Tyler, had died just a few months ago, Matthew appearing at his front door was the best thing that had happened to him in a long time.

"Would you like to go for a walk?" Liam said, pointing to a big hill several miles from them. "There's an awesome view over the national park."

"Sure. Let's go," Matthew said. "Let me just get my backpack."

"We can leave our stuff here. It's only two hours or something from here."

Matthew emerged from the tent carrying his backpack. "I don't want anybody to steal my stuff."

"As you wish, but it looks quite heavy. Don't expect me to carry it."

"You're such a great friend. I can't even remember how many times I have carried your bag or bike or whatever."

"Nice try. Won't work."

They followed the river nearly two miles and then took a path that crossed a small forest. Soon, they came to a lake, which was between two crags. They sat on a bench near the path, and Liam took a drink from the water bottle he had been carrying at his waist. He offered it to Matthew, who was sweating.

"Hey, leave some for me, too," he said when Matthew kept drinking.

"Um, sorry," Matthew said and looked down. "I just…," he began, but the words trailed off.

Liam took the bottle and drank what little was left at the bottom. Hoping there was fresh water in the spring to fill the bottle, he attached the empty water bottle back to his belt.

"You were about to say something," Liam said.

"Hmm, it's nothing," Matthew said, still avoiding Liam's eyes.

"You can tell me if something is bothering you," Liam said. "Best friends forever, right?" he added.

They watched as a flock of geese landed on the water. Liam found it funny how their feet touched the water like the landing gear of an airplane. Matthew stayed quiet and stared at the birds.

"Can I ask you something?" he said finally.

Liam turned to look at him. "Sure."

"Were you already gay when we lived in Grand Rapids?"

I've always been gay, Liam thought but decided not to start lecturing on the topic. Besides, Matthew seemed to be cool about it.

"Yes. I was already gay," he said.

"Did you have a crush on me?" Matthew asked and looked Liam in the eyes.

Chapter 6

Alex ate breakfast with Coach Hanson in the canteen. It was Wednesday, the third day of swim camp. Alex rested his head on his hands and fluffed his hair. He stopped when he noticed that Roy was glaring at him.

I'm not going to let that idiot win, Alex thought and took a better position on his chair.

The previous day had been a disaster. First thing in the morning, Alex had tried to apologize to Roy for the stupid comment about his erection in the shower. As he should have known, talking about it was the last thing the jock wanted to do. Instead, Roy had spent the whole day sabotaging every single training session.

The backstroke theory lesson had been the worst. If Roy wasn't disagreeing with everything Alex said, he was spending his energy asking childish questions. Under other circumstances, Alex might have found the comment about gays swimming bare-backstroke funny, but when mentioned in the classroom, it had only made him blush.

And then there was the other thing. Liam hadn't answered his calls or called back for two days. Every time he tried to call, it went straight to voicemail.

I've sent him a hundred text messages. Why can't he just reply and at least let me know he's okay? Alex bemoaned. He tried to calm himself down with the thought that Liam's parents would have called him for sure if something had happened. Still, it wasn't typical for Liam to neglect Alex's calls.

"Something bothering you?" Coach Hanson asked.

"Is it that obvious?" Alex said and forced a smile on his face. "It's just that Liam hasn't answered my calls."

Alex didn't want to tell the coach about Roy. It was something he wanted to handle by himself. He had to, if he ever wanted to become a coach.

"Oh. You've been arguing," Coach said with a fatherly smile. "Young love. Can be spicy," he added.

"It's nothing like that," Alex said. Liam sometimes sulked over something Alex didn't even know he had done wrong, but Alex was pretty sure this time it was something different. *If he still doesn't answer, I'll call his parents this evening.*

"You could take your group to the sports field until lunch," Coach Hanson said. "There is a ball in the trunk of my car if you want to play soccer."

Alex sighed. Being alone with the boys, especially with Roy, half a mile from the swim center, didn't sound like a tempting idea. Still, he found himself nodding to the coach.

Coach Hanson sipped what was left of his coffee and stood up. "Have fun," he said and punched Alex on his shoulder. "I'll take my boys to the pool."

One command from the coach was enough, and the boys who belonged to his group rushed out of the canteen to change into their speedos. Alex finished his oatmeal and asked the rest of the boys to prepare to leave.

"Yes, ma'am," Roy replied, "but we'll finish our breakfast first."

"We're leaving now. Be in front of the building in five," Alex said and left to fetch the soccer ball.

Ten minutes later, even Roy had joined the others, and the group started walking toward the sports field. The younger boys talked enthusiastically with each other, which gave Alex some hope that this would become a better day.

"Okay. Let's run two laps around the track," Alex said and put the soccer ball down.

"That's boring. Why don't we just play?" Roy shouted.

"Because I said we run first," Alex replied.

"Who cares what you say?" Roy glared at Alex and mouthed "faggot."

Alex pondered his options while the rest of the group stared at him. The smirk on Roy's face was growing wider, which made Alex's blood boil again. This time, he, however, took a couple breaths to calm down before he opened his mouth.

"You don't have to participate if you don't want," Alex said, "but I'll tell the coach, and he'll send you home," he continued.

"Sissy runs to papa. How scary," Roy kept mocking.

"Roy, don't be childish," Luke said. "Let's go," he added and began running. The rest of the boys followed him, even Roy.

Alex took out his phone and checked his messages, but there was nothing from Liam. He knew his boyfriend liked to sleep late, but he still tried to call Liam. Again, it went to voicemail.

Why the hell won't you answer me? Alex began typing an angry message, but at the last moment, he deleted it. *Fine. He must have something better to do than talk to me.*

The boys had nearly finished the first lap and were approaching him. Roy was twenty yards behind the others, and it looked like he was limping on his left leg.

"My leg hurts. Can I stop running, Coach?" he shouted.

"Do whatever you want," Alex said.

"What? You're not telling Papa?"

"Look, Roy, you're not training for me. You're training to become a great athlete. It's up to you what you want."

Alex turned his back to Roy, took the ball, and walked to the soccer field. In his mind, he repeated the words he had just said to Roy, and a satisfied smile rose on his face. Even Coach Hanson couldn't have handled the situation better. When he turned to look a moment later, Roy had reached the other boys.

When the boys had finished the second lap, Alex split them into two teams. He threw the ball to the field, and he didn't even have to ask them to start playing.

"This is not just about swimming. We came here to have fun and spend time together." Alex remembered Coach Hanson's words on the first day they had arrived. They still surprised him. *Jeez, the man is getting older and softer*, he thought.

Alex watched the soccer game for a while before his thoughts drifted back to Liam. He tried to call his boyfriend one more time. When he failed again, Alex called Mrs. Green, who answered almost immediately.

"Oh. He didn't tell you," Mrs. Green said and explained where Liam was.

"Will Liam be back home by Friday?" Alex asked.

"I have Friday off, and I'll pick them up from the park in the morning," she said.

Alex thanked her for the info and ended the call. He browsed the messages that he had sent to Liam. Some of them were a bit edgy, but thankfully, he hadn't written anything too stupid. Liam would understand.

But why on earth didn't he tell me he had met his childhood friend? Alex pondered. Liam didn't typically hide things from him. Alex put his phone back in his pocket so he wouldn't write a message he would regret afterward.

An hour later, Alex decided the boys had played enough. He wanted to take them back to the swim center and continue their lessons on swimming technique. When he approached the soccer field, Roy tried to make a goal but missed, and the ball came toward him.

"Okay, time to get back! Let's meet in the auditorium in half an hour," Alex said with a loud voice and picked up the ball.

The sweaty but smiling boys left jogging toward the swim center. Not even Roy was objecting this time, which was a pleasant surprise. The jock talked casually with some other boys, and when his eyes met with Alex's, the expression on his face didn't change.

Brandon, instead, lingered on the soccer field. Once the other boys were far enough, he approached Alex. His hair and forehead were wet, and he seemed to have difficulty making eye contact with Alex. Finally, he began to speak tentatively.

"Um … you had a boyfriend in high school," he said.

Alex assumed it was a question. "Yes, I did. We're still together."

"I have … a friend who is … gay. I mean, I think he might be."

"Does that concern you?"

Brandon looked at Alex. His eyes were big, and he replied quickly. "No. No. I don't mind at all. It's okay. Really."

Alex smiled at the boy, which seemed to calm him down. Alex looked at him and nodded to encourage Brandon to continue.

"I was just wondering if you could give me some advice about what I should do," he said. "I would like to support him."

"Sure," Alex said. "Let's talk after the supper. Okay?"

The smile on Brandon's face grew broader. He thanked Alex and ran after his friends toward the swim center to take a shower before the next lesson. Alex followed him, thinking that, whoever Brandon's friend was, he was lucky to have such a good friend.

"Any questions?" Alex asked to finish the lesson.

"Actually, I have one," Roy said. "How do you swim if your wrists are limp?"

Aw, Jesus, could he be any more childish? Alex thought. "See you after lunch at the pool," he said and waited until everybody had left the small auditorium.

Luke gave him a sympathetic look, and Alex smiled at him. It was a welcomed reminder that most of the kids on the swim team were openminded and didn't give a shit what he was or wasn't. Then there was this one bad apple who, now and then, made Alex wish swim camp would end.

After lunch, Alex went to the locker room to change his clothes. Most of the boys were already there. Roy was standing on the other side of the room, naked, his back to Alex.

Nice ass, man, Alex thought but, at the last moment, he decided not to say it aloud. After all, he didn't want to sink to the bully's level.

"Hey, Coach, what are we practicing next?" Luke asked.

Alex turned to look at the door, but Coach Hanson wasn't there. Then he realized Luke was talking to him.

"Um, backstroke mostly," Alex said.

From the corner of his eye, Alex saw Roy putting on his speedo quickly. Then he hurried out of the locker room. Alex avoided his gaze at first, but as soon as his back disappeared, Alex rushed to the corridor.

"Roy!" he shouted.

The jock stopped and turned around. He stared at Alex and frowned.

"Let's talk," Alex said and opened a door that led to a small office.

Roy followed him into the office and closed the door. They were standing in the small room with only a few yards between them. Alex was still dressed in a t-shirt and shorts; Roy had on nothing but his speedo.

"It's time to stop this bullshit," Alex said, and his face was severe. "Either you start behaving, or I'll send you home."

After staring at Alex for several seconds, Roy finally said, "Fine."

"I can see you've got a lot of talent. You've got a fair chance of getting a scholarship if you focus your energy on training," Alex said.

When Roy didn't say anything, Alex offered him a hand. "Truce?"

"Truce," Roy muttered. He didn't meet Alex's eye but still shook his hand.

"Okay, good. Off you go, then," Alex said.

Roy left without saying a word, and Alex returned to the locker room to get dressed. Luke smiled at him when they met at the locker room door. Probably, he had heard his discussion with Roy.

Alex walked to the pool with new confidence. His back was straight, and the look in his eyes was calm when he counted that everybody was there. Then he asked the boys to stand in a row next to the first lane.

"Okay, let's practice backstroke start," he said and pointed at Roy. "You're first. Take the starting position."

Roy sighed but jumped into the water. Alex followed him, and soon they were at the end of the lane. Roy was holding on the metal bar with his hands, and his feet were on the ledge attached to the wall. Alex was between Roy and the line divider, so close their bodies almost touched each other.

"Everybody, look here," he shouted to the boys. "This is a very good starting position," he said and took hold of Roy's ankle.

Roy glared at him but straightened his head quickly when he saw the determination in Alex's eyes. Alex tried to hide his smile when he rested his left hand on Roy's shoulder.

"You get the best power when your feet are where your shoulders are. Too narrow or too wide and you're gonna lose some strength," Alex explained to the boys who were standing by the pool.

"Okay, take your mark," Alex said.

Roy pulled himself out of the water. Alex moved a bit farther to see better. *The guy is really good when he takes this seriously*, he thought.

"That's very good," Alex said. "As you can see, Roy's butt is over the top of the water. That requires quite a lot of strength, but it's the fastest way to start."

Alex asked Roy to launch and do ten kicks before returning to the side of the pool to wait for his next turn. They practiced a couple of rounds, after which Alex took three of the boys to the second lane to give them more guidance. He asked the rest of the group to swim back and forth in the first lane.

The training session lasted almost two hours before Alex asked the boys to hit the showers. He detached the backstroke ledges and brought them back to the equipment room before he joined the boys in the shower room.

"You did really well," Alex said to Roy as he took the showerhead next to him.

Roy didn't reply. He finished washing his hair and vanished to the locker room. *Fair enough. It was a truce, not a peace treaty*, Alex thought. At least the practice had gone fine without additional incidents, which was more than he had hoped.

As they had agreed, Brandon came to talk to Alex after supper. They found cozy armchairs in the lobby, which was silent as the other boys had left the building. Brandon looked so small in the big chair when he set his hands on the armrests.

"I think you were very brave. Coming out at Fairmont High and dating your boyfriend," Brandon said. "At least, that's what I've heard," he added.

Alex studied Brandon carefully but couldn't remember seeing him in high school. Probably the boy had just finished his freshman year, and they had never studied there at the same time.

"Oh. I didn't know they were still talking about me at school," Alex said.

"Sure they are. You're the best swimmer we've ever had," Brandon said, raising his voice. He lowered it again, almost whispering, "Well, and then there are those rumors they keep telling in the locker room. I didn't believe them before what you said on Monday."

"You didn't believe that a jock could be gay," Alex said and laughed.

Brandon blushed. He took hold of the armrests and leaned away from Alex. "Sorry, I didn't—"

"I didn't believe it either," Alex said. "Besides, I wasn't brave."

With a confused look on his face, Brandon studied Alex. "How did you meet your boyfriend?"

"It was a coincidence. Our history teacher, Mr. Timothy, paired us for an assignment," Alex said. "I had known for some time that I might be gay, but it wasn't until Liam and I became friends that I started to think I could date a guy."

I had already decided that I would never date anyone. Alex felt lucky that his plan hadn't actualized. A small smile appeared on his face when he thought about the warm autumn weekends he and Liam had spent walking hand-in-hand in the big parks near campus.

"Were your parents cool with it?" Brandon asked.

Alex shook his head, and his face grew severe. Since his mother had died soon after he'd told her, they'd never had a chance to talk about it properly. His father's opinion he knew, far too well. *I don't have parents. Not anymore.*

"So, you have a friend and you think he's gay," Alex said to change to topic.

"Huh? Yes," Brandon said. He placed his hands under his thighs, sitting on them.

"What makes you think so?"

"I think he doesn't find girls attractive."

"So, is he more interested in looking at other boys?"

Brandon nodded and looked at Alex with his big brown eyes. He had blushed a bit, in a way that Alex found cute.

Alex scanned the lobby to check they were still alone. "There's no friend, and we're talking about you, aren't we?" he said in a low voice.

The red color on Brandon's face got deeper. "Could you please not tell anybody?" he asked. His voice was shaking.

"Of course I won't tell anyone," Alex said. He leaned toward the boy and patted his shoulder. "Have you spoken to your parents?"

"No!" Brandon raised his voice. "My mom and aunt are constantly asking if I have found a girlfriend. They would be so disappointed."

Alex saw Brandon's sad face, and he wished he could tell the boy that everything was okay and that his family would understand. That might be the case, but his own experience was unfortunate proof that things could go wrong, too.

"What do I do?" Brandon said and stared at Alex with his beautiful eyes, which began to fill with tears.

"Come here," Alex said and stood. He wrapped his arms around the crying boy. "Everything's gonna be okay. I promise."

Alex didn't know how he could keep that promise, but those words felt best in the situation. He hoped he could figure out something.

He was unaware that Roy was watching them behind the glass door and taking pictures of their hug with his phone. When Alex and Brandon left the lobby a few minutes later, Roy had already gone to his room.

Chapter 7

Matthew looked at his friend and waited for an answer to the question that had been bothering him for years.

Liam blushed. "Let's keep going," he said and was about to stand up.

"Did you have a crush on me?" Matthew asked again.

"I did," Liam said finally.

Matthew felt tightness in his chest, and his face grew severe. He stood and kicked the flowers that were growing near the path. *I was so stupid. I should've known*, he thought.

"Matthew, please look at me," Liam said. "Don't be worried. I know you're straight, and I'm dating Alex."

Liam stared at him and wiggled his legs. Matthew couldn't help smiling at him. It was the same Liam he had known since they were toddlers. *I wish things had gone differently*, Matthew thought.

"So, are we good?" Liam asked.

"Yeah. Friends forever," Matthew said. It felt so bittersweet.

With a broad smile on his face, Liam stood up. They were standing close to each other, and Matthew pondered whether this was a moment when they were meant to hug each other. By the time he made up his mind, Liam was already on the path waiting for him.

They walked fifteen minutes in silence, enjoying the national park. When they were young, they used to wander in the forests all the time. It was the first time in years Matthew had strolled around in nature breathing fresh air.

It's a bit different in Memphis. Matthew tried to enjoy the break from his ordinary life, which he didn't want to think right now.

"Tell me something about Alex," he said. "How did you guys meet each other?"

"Huh? Well, it was our history teacher who paired us for an assignment. Then we became friends," Liam said.

"How convenient," Matthew said. "In Alabama, we didn't have a gay dating service at the high school."

Liam laughed. "Fairmont High is a full-service school," he said.

"So, first you were friends, and then you began banging each other."

There was a meaningful look on Liam's face. Matthew was sure Liam knew he was just giving his friend a hard time. Liam got embarrassed so easily that sometimes Matthew felt guilty for teasing him. On the other hand, it was a lot of fun, and Liam would get payback as soon as the opportunity arose.

"I'll spare you the details, but if you really want to know, yes, we have had sex a couple times," Liam said with a smile on his face.

For sure more than a couple times, Matthew thought. Talking about his friend's sex life gave him mixed feelings.

There was one discussion, several years ago, that he remembered vividly. They had been twelve or something, and Liam had told him that one day he would marry a pretty girl and have two children. Apparently, the plan had changed.

"Are you seeing someone?" Liam asked.

"No," Matthew said quickly. "I want to get my … I mean, I want to finish my studies and get a proper job first."

"Sounds like a plan," Liam said. "Although you never know when you'll meet the right one. Life can be full of surprises," he added.

I couldn't agree more, Matthew thought and kept walking.

Soon, they got to the edge of the forest. Matthew followed Liam down a steep slope, taking hold of the trees here and there to keep from falling. At the bottom, they found the spring, and Liam filled the water bottle.

"Give me some. My mouth is drier than sandpaper," Matthew said.

"Who said you needed to carry that backpack?" Liam said and handed him the bottle.

Jesus, this is so good, Matthew thought, and soon the bottle was empty again. He moved his shoulders back and forth to prevent the dizzy feeling that tried to take over his head.

"Do we have any food?" he asked.

Liam took an energy bar from his pocket. "Here. As you can see, I'm well prepared," he said and smiled.

Easy for you to say when you have everything, Matthew thought and took a bite of the bar.

He wasn't jealous of Liam—or maybe he was a bit—but it was his own situation that frustrated him. Sooner or later, he had to travel back to Memphis, or somewhere else. *Unless*....

"Are you ready to continue?" Liam asked.

Matthew awakened from his thoughts. "Huh? What? Yes."

"We just need to climb on top of that hill, and we are there."

With some new energy in his muscles, Matthew managed to get to the top of the hill. As soon as he got there, he sat down on the ground and tried to calm his breathing. He could feel his heart beating stronger than normally.

"Come on! Take a look at this view," Liam shouted.

"Just give me a minute. I need to relax," Matthew said and bent his legs.

Liam walked to him. "Are you okay?" he asked.

Matthew felt how the blood was flowing back to his head, which made him feel better. His pulse was still fast, and he felt an emerging headache on his forehead.

"I'm okay. Just a bit tired," he said, forcing a smile on his face. "Apparently, I'm not used to walking this much."

A couple minutes later, Matthew stood up, and Liam described how the national park continued on the other side of the hill. As far as they could see, there were forests and lakes.

We're really in the middle of nowhere, Matthew thought when his phone began ringing in the backpack. He had a bad feeling about it, but he still opened the side pocket to get the phone.

"Oh. There is a network in here," Liam said. "Shame that I didn't bring my phone with me."

"Hey, sis," Matthew said dryly and walked farther away to talk with her.

Maria got straight to business. "Where are you?"

"You know I'm not going to tell you that," Matthew said.

"Please, trust me this time," Maria said, but when Matthew stayed quiet, she continued, "I just wanted to tell you that Mom and Dad are looking for you."

"I don't give a shit. Tell me something I don't know."

"They suspect you're in Fairmont."

Matthew's heart skipped a beat. Without goodbyes, he ended the call and switched off the home. Then he saw Liam, who had a confused look on his face.

Fuck. I wonder how much he heard.

This is so unfair, Matthew thought as he rushed past the narrow path that led to the spring and continued toward their camp, as far as he could remember the route. Liam followed him and kept asking him to stop, but Matthew couldn't. Everything was ruined; that was the story of his life.

"I don't want to talk about it," Matthew yelled and walked faster.

"Let's not talk then," Liam shouted. "But you could still wait for me. Please."

Matthew stopped. He heard his friend's heavy breathing as he approached him. When Liam got there, Matthew looked at him and saw a face that told him—without a single word—that everything would be okay. It wasn't true, but for a short moment, Matthew wanted to believe that it was.

"I take it you want to get back to the camp," Liam said in a soft voice that was full of compassion.

"Yes, please," Matthew said, and those were his only words until they arrived at their tent.

Liam began preparing lunch, and Matthew walked to the riverbank. Water on the river was flowing slowly, without a worry about how to survive until the next morning. Matthew moved closer to the water and wondered how deep it would be in the middle of the river.

What if I just walked there and let it take me to a better place? he thought. It felt so tempting.

He took the first step and felt how his sneakers became wet. He had always hated the feeling, but now it didn't matter. His miserable life would end here, and nobody would long for him.

Liam has his boyfriend. Mom and Dad would be happier if I didn't exist, he thought. All that despair and hopelessness rushed through his body and pushed him deeper into the water. The surface of the water touched his shorts and colored them darker.

Matthew began feeling dizzy, and it required more and more effort to keep from falling—but did it really matter if he fell? Wasn't that the whole purpose of him being there?

I need to get farther, he thought and took a careful step. Despite the slippery rocks at the bottom of the river, he managed to stand. The water was already up to his crotch.

"What on earth are you doing?" Liam shouted, standing on the bank.

It was when he turned to look at his friend that Matthew fell. His head went under the water, and he floundered with his arms to reach the surface. It wasn't until he felt Liam's hand touching his that he realized he had wanted to drown and not to be saved.

With a surprising amount of determination, Liam pulled him to shore. His eyes, which typically smiled, were filled with concern. His hands took hold of Matthew's head and turned it so he could see that Matthew was still alive.

"Did you just try to kill yourself?" Liam asked, shocked.

Matthew looked Liam in the eyes and felt, for the first time in a long time, that somebody might actually care about him—and not just anybody, but Liam.

Matthew tried to smile carefully. "Thanks for saving me. I didn't realize how deep it was there," he said.

The worry on Liam's face changed to confusion. "What were you doing there in the first place?"

"Just wanted to see if there were any fish."

The expression on Liam's face made it clear he didn't buy the explanation.

"I know. It was stupid. Can we just not talk about it?" Matthew said.

"Okay. There are a lot of things you don't want to talk about today."

The guilt caused by his friend's words was ice in Matthew's guts. Despite the warm weather, he felt frozen inside. There was only one cure, and he had to get his medicine soon, or his world would collapse.

"Lunch is ready," Liam said. "Would you like to at least eat something?"

"Yeah, I just need to take a leak first," Matthew said.

It was a lie, again, but why would it matter? This whole trip and him being there with his former friend in the middle of the forest was just one big lie. Nothing he said would give him what he wanted.

Matthew took his backpack and walked behind the same bushes he'd used that morning. After checking that Liam couldn't see him, he opened the side pocket and took out the plastic bag. He grimaced when he realized how few pills were left.

He took a molly in his hand and studied it for a moment as if it were his best friend. Then he swallowed it like he had done countless times before. The synthetic methamphetamine would kick in soon and save his day. At least, that was what Matthew hoped.

The savior came, and soon all his worries where replaced by chemical warmth and happiness. Had anybody told him those feelings were not real, Matthew would have called him a liar.

Matthew returned to the tent where Liam was waiting for him with lunch. "Oh, honey, that smells so delicious," Matthew said, unable to keep the broad grin from his face.

"I hope it tastes good, too," Liam said tentatively and studied his friend.

"I'm sure it does. You're such a fantastic cook."

Rolling his eyes, Liam offered him a plate, which was filled with cooked rice, fried vegetables, and canned tuna. Matthew wasn't only hungry, but the food was actually pretty good. Everything Liam did was good.

I would be dating that sexy, good-looking guy if my fucking idiot mother hadn't ruined everything, Matthew thought but tried to push it out of his mind. Maybe it wasn't too late yet.

Chapter 8

It was Thursday afternoon, the last day of the camping trip before Liam's mother would pick them up the following morning. The sun was shining, but Liam didn't feel happy and relaxed. He kept watching Matthew, who was sitting on the riverbank throwing small rocks into the water.

What if he has some mental illness?

The last thing Liam remembered Matthew's mother telling him was that Matthew was sick and couldn't see him. Then the whole family had moved away.

Maybe they moved so he could get treatment, and he's just too ashamed to tell me about it, Liam thought.

But, that didn't make much sense. As far as Liam could remember, Matthew had been a typical high school kid. Now his friend's mood kept changing constantly. The Matthew sitting on the riverbank wasn't the same boy who used to be his best friend, and Liam wanted more than anything to know what had happened.

"Can I sit here?" Liam asked. He sat next to Matthew and noticed his eyes were teary. "Is something wrong?"

Matthew wiped the tears and smiled. "I just miss those days when we were friends in Grand Rapids," he said.

"Me, too."

How do you ask someone if he's mentally ill? Liam pondered but couldn't find a way that wouldn't potentially hurt Matthew's feelings. That was a risk Liam didn't want to take. His friend was fragile enough even without additional provocation.

"I lied to you about why we moved to Fairmont," Liam said. "It wasn't because of my dad's job."

Matthew turned to look at him. For a moment, Liam saw his old friend in the curious but understanding expression on his face.

"After you left, I didn't have any friends. Mom and Dad thought I would be better off in Fairmont," Liam said.

A tear rolled down Matthew's cheek. He sobbed about how sorry he was that he had left without saying a word and had not contacted Liam before now. Liam put his arm around his friend's shoulder. Soon, Matthew's head rested against his shoulder.

"I didn't mean to blame you. It's not your fault that your aunt got sick," Liam said and petted Matthew's shoulder.

"I haven't been fully honest about one thing either," Matthew said.

Liam held his breath and hoped he would finally learn what was wrong with his friend.

"I had a big argument with my mother," Matthew said.

"Is that why you left and came to Fairmont?" Liam asked.

"Um, yes," Matthew said. "Of course, I wanted to see you, too," he added quickly.

"What was the argument about?"

Matthew was quiet for a long time, watching the river. Several times, he opened his mouth to say something but closed it before any words came out. Liam went through different options in his mind while waiting patiently for his friend to continue.

"It was about school," Matthew said finally.

"She would like you to finish high school?"

"Yes."

"But … didn't you want that, too?" Liam asked. He couldn't understand why Matthew would argue with his mom about something when they were on the same side.

"It's a long story. Can we talk about something else?" Matthew asked.

"We have nothing but time. Please, tell me," Liam tried to push his friend.

"I said I don't want to talk about it!" Matthew yelled and stood up. His breathing was heavy, and he stared at Liam when he repeated, "I don't want to talk about it. Understood?"

Startled, Liam sat and watched when Matthew raced along the path to the forest and disappeared. He couldn't remember his friend ever behaving like that.

There is something wrong. We need to get out of here, Liam thought and walked to the tent. He switched on his phone and tried, in vain, to find the network. Frustrated, he put the phone back. Walking to the hill would have been an option, but Matthew might come back while he was away.

I can't leave him alone like that, Liam decided. The memory of Matthew walking into the river fully dressed was too vivid in his mind.

Liam searched almost an hour, but Matthew was nowhere to be found. Even if he heard his calls, he didn't answer. Liam walked along the riverbank to check if there were footsteps on the sand. There weren't, which was probably a good sign.

What should I do next? What would Dad do? Or Alex?

"Matthew! Please come here!" he shouted as loud as he could. It hurt his throat, but he tried again. And a third time, but nobody answered.

The sun began to set, and his friend was alone in the forest without a flashlight. One more time, Liam walked along the path to the forest calling Matthew, but his friend had decided to disappear.

What the heck should I do? Liam asked himself. Finally, he realized he could at least set the campfire. If the darkness came before Matthew returned, the fire could guide him back to the tent. Liam congratulated himself for the idea and began collecting wood. When the fire was set, he hoped Matthew would see it, if he even wanted to come back.

Darkness filled the clearing where they had set the tent. Liam added more and more wood to the campfire, trying to make it as big as possible. He kept calling his friend, but it began to feel pointless.

Fucking idiot, Liam cursed but regretted his thoughts. *What if Matthew really is ill? And now he's somewhere and needs my help? Or worse, what if he's dead and it's all my fault?*

The more he thought about it, the more convinced he became that he had to walk to the hill and call for help. The idea of walking alone two hours in the pitch-dark forest wasn't especially tempting, but something inside him said he had to do it. Besides, Liam was sure Matthew would have done the same for him. *Friends forever.*

Liam went to the tent to get his flashlight. He switched it on and saw Matthew's backpack in the spotlight.

Should I check his bag first? He might have some medicine there. That info might help the rescue team, Liam thought. He opened the backpack and began taking Matthew's clothes out of it. He checked it with the flashlight but, other than the clothes, the backpack was empty.

He had just opened the zipper of the side pocket when he heard some noise. He turned to look and saw Matthew's face peeking inside the tent. A dried trail of blood went from his forehead along his nose.

"Hi, honey. Did you miss me already?" Matthew said cheerfully. Then he saw that Liam had emptied his backpack. He rushed inside the tent and crammed his clothes into the backpack.

"Don't touch my pack!" he roared.

"Relax," Liam said. "I was just trying to—"

"Never touch my backpack," Matthew said slowly, emphasizing each word. He stared at Liam, his eyes scary.

"What's wrong with you?" Liam whispered. "You're not the same Matthew I used to know."

Matthew froze. Slowly, he let go of the backpack and crawled out of the tent. Liam rushed to the door to see if his friend would run to the forest again. He was relieved when he saw him in the dim light of the campfire.

Should I go to talk to him? Liam wondered. The entire situation began to frustrate him, and he wished it was already morning and his mother was picking them up.

Matthew's mysterious backpack was lying unguarded on his friend's sleeping bag. Liam couldn't understand why Matthew had gone ballistic when he had taken the clothes out of it. On the other hand, his behavior hadn't been the most rational lately.

Unless he's hiding something, Liam thought and took his flashlight.

Trying not to make a sound, Liam checked that Matthew was still sitting by the campfire. Then he approached the backpack carefully, hoping he would find something. At the same time, he didn't want to find anything.

Holding his breath, Liam opened the zipper of the side pocket and pushed his hand inside. There was something plastic. He pulled out a small zip-lock bag that contained colorful pills.

Oh my god … these are not medicine, Liam thought and looked at the pills, which had smiling faces. Those were supposed to look happy, but for him, the smirk was evil.

Liam heard some noise outside and shoved the bag back into the side pocket. Taking a good position on his side of the tent, he prepared for Matthew to step inside. That didn't happen, but Liam noticed his armpits were sweating. For the first time in his life, he wasn't afraid for Matthew. He was afraid of him.

He's using drugs, Liam thought and covered his face with his hands. *Why didn't I realize it immediately? And what do I do now?*

Suddenly, he remembered the pocket knife.

I need to find it, Liam thought. He searched the other side pockets of Matthew's backpack, twice, but couldn't find it. *Matthew must have taken it.*

Half an hour later, Liam was still sitting in the tent. He didn't want to sleep because of what Matthew could do to him or to himself. Going out and facing Matthew didn't sound tempting either.

"Liam?" He heard Matthew's voice outside. It was quiet, soft, even friendly.

"Yes," Liam replied hesitantly.

"Could you come here? Please."

Slowly, Liam crawled out of the tent and saw his friend sitting near the campfire, which was gradually dying down. As much as he could see in the dim light,

Matthew was smiling at him. Liam added a couple logs to the fire and sat down.

"There's something I should tell you," Matthew said and looked down. "You're not going to like it."

"I saw the pills," Liam said.

"I'm so sorry," Matthew said, and tears began rolling down his cheeks.

Liam just stared at him, feeling numb. He couldn't understand why Matthew had become a drug addict. No matter how much he had wanted to, he just couldn't tell his friend that everything would be fine. The Matthew he had once liked—and liked a lot— didn't exist anymore.

"The knife," Liam said and held out his hand.

"What?" Matthew asked and knitted his brows. "You can't possibly believe that I … that I would hurt you."

"Give it to me," Liam said.

Without further objection, Matthew took the knife from his pocket and passed it to Liam, who threw it into the river. Matthew looked at him with his mouth open, but one meaningful look from Liam was enough to shut it.

Liam's head was full of questions, but only one of them was important. He turned to look at his friend and waited until their eyes met.

"Why?" he said.

Matthew turned his head immediately away. "You wouldn't understand."

"Try me." This time, Liam wasn't going to give up.

"I can't," Matthew said with a voice hardly louder than a whisper. "You wouldn't want to be my friend anymore."

"For God's sake. If you don't tell me right here, right now, I will never want to see you again," Liam said, raising his voice.

Matthew winced. He looked at Liam, and his eyes were big and full of terror. "You can't mean that," he said.

"When did you start to use drugs?" Liam said as calmly as he could.

"After we moved to Russellville," Matthew said and sighed. "You weren't there, and I ended up hanging around with the wrong guys."

"So, is it my fault?" Liam said.

"No!" Matthew said quickly. "I just mean that I missed you, and I didn't have any friends."

Having been lonely after Matthew's family moved away, Liam understood far too well what his friend meant. Of course, he didn't approve of Matthew's actions, but being angry at him became harder and harder.

"Would you help me get rid of that stuff?" Matthew asked.

"We'll take you to a rehab center first thing on Monday morning," Liam said and rested his hand on his friend's shoulder.

"Thanks," Matthew said and sat quietly for a moment. Then he said, "I would appreciate if we didn't tell your parents."

"Okay. Fine," Liam said.

He didn't like the idea of keeping it secret from his parents, but if that was the price he had to pay to detoxify his friend, he was willing to pay it. One thing was still sure: He would tell Alex. Keeping in mind what secrets used to do to their relationship, that was non-negotiable.

"Thanks, Liam. You're the best," Matthew said and turned to hug him.

Liam squeezed Matthew hard. All this felt like the first sign of new hope that he might get his friend back. It felt real and honest, and neither of them wanted to let go. When they did, Liam's eyes were moist, and so were Matthew's.

"Let's try to get some sleep," Liam said. "It's an early wake-up tomorrow."

They went to the tent and crawled inside their sleeping bags. Matthew was about to reach the lantern to switch it off when Liam stopped him.

"I'm really glad you told me," Liam said.

Matthew nodded him and gave a shy smile. Then he pressed the button, and darkness fell in the tent. Happy thoughts filled Liam's mind when he closed his eyes and fell asleep soon after.

Half an hour later, peaceful snoring came from Liam's side of the tent. On the opposite side, Matthew was awake, staring at the roof even though he couldn't see it in the darkness. Slowly, his hand moved toward the backpack and opened the zipper. He took a pill—the last one, he promised himself—and swallowed it. Then he closed his eyes.

The sun was already beginning to rise above the horizon when Liam suddenly woke up. Something touched his face. It took a moment to realize that Matthew was kissing him.

Liam pulled his head away. "What are—?" he managed to say before Matthew interrupted him.

"You're so beautiful," he said with a friendly smile on his face.

Chapter 9

"I need to talk to you," Coach Hanson said to Alex, who had just arrived in the cafeteria for breakfast.

They went to the empty auditorium. As soon as the coach sat on the corner of the table, Alex recognized the expression on his face. The man had some important news to tell.

"We're getting guests from the Swimming Coaches Association next week," he said.

"Okay. But why?" Alex asked.

"They're from Eddington, looking for a part-time coach to help at the high schools there."

It didn't take long for Alex to realize he was referring to him. Had the coach really arranged a job interview for him? And how did Coach Hanson know that he was interested in becoming a swim coach?

Liam is behind all this, Alex realized. Even if the coach calling him and offering him a job at the camp had been one big coincidence, the headhunters from Eddington suddenly appearing there was far too much.

"I see," Alex said. "The little birds have been telling you things."

"There are no birds here," the coach said. "I just thought you would like to coach high school kids."

"I'm so not buying that."

Coach Hanson laughed. "Okay. Fair enough. I might have had a couple of phone calls with Mrs. Green," he said. "By the way, she seems very nice."

Yes, she is. And so is her son, Alex thought with a satisfied smile on his face. He made a mental note to thank them both as soon as he got to Fairmont in the evening.

"So, are you interested, or should I cancel their visit?" Coach Hanson asked.

"I think I might be," Alex said, grinning. "Thanks, Coach."

There was a fatherly expression on Coach Hanson's face when he looked at Alex. He had raised a great athlete and felt proud that Alex would follow his footsteps.

"One more thing," he said when Alex was leaving the auditorium. "Could you take the kids to the pool and get them started? I've got some errands to run in the city."

"Yes, sir."

Unable to hide his smile, Alex hurried to the canteen to get some breakfast before the first training session.

For the first time, he would be responsible for the entire swim team. *This is awesome! Liam deserves a big kiss.*

Half an hour later, Alex was standing by the pool blowing the whistle and shouting lap times to the boys. Soon, he noticed everything came quite naturally. Most of the time, he was following the example of how Coach Hanson had managed the trainings when he had been on the team.

Alex kept a special eye on Roy since he was worried that the boy would cause trouble. However, so far, the bad-tempered jock had listened to all his instructions and done what was asked.

Maybe the truce will turn into a ceasefire before camp is over, Alex thought hopefully.

A few minutes before training finished, Coach Hanson called Alex. His business in Buonas had taken longer than he had expected, and he asked if Alex could coach the boys the rest of the day. Alex happily agreed and wished the coach a nice weekend.

Each year, as part of the swim camp program, there was a swimming competition with swimmers from other high schools in the area. Coach Hanson had typically managed to get athletic department leaders from different colleges to follow the competition. Now there seemed to be some logistical challenges, and Alex hoped the coach would be able to sort them out. These kids definitely deserved the chance to demonstrate their skills.

Alex told the boys to get out of the pool, and before they headed to the shower, he told them Coach Hanson would join them on Monday. He didn't like the smirk

118

on Roy's face when he said it. However, taking into account how well the morning session had gone, he was confident everything would go okay in the afternoon, too.

After lunch, Alex joined the boys in the pool. They practiced different strokes: freestyle, breaststroke, butterfly, and backstroke. Coach Hanson had asked him to think about who the two best candidates would be to represent Fairmont High in the swimming competition the following week.

By the time training ended, Alex had made up his mind. He would propose Luke and Roy to the coach. There were other good swimmers on the team, but those two had the most potential.

"Okay, hit the showers," Alex said. "See you in the auditorium in thirty minutes. We'll wrap up the week, and then it's time to go home."

After the other boys had gone inside the building, Brandon approached Alex. "Do you have a minute?" he asked.

"Sure. What's on your mind?" Alex said.

"I've been thinking," Brandon said and kept a long pause. "I think I'll come out to my parents this weekend."

"Uh-oh. That's a big decision. Are you sure?"

Brandon nodded. "It scares the crap out of me," he admitted.

"I'm sure it does," Alex said. "Let me know if I can help you somehow."

They went to the empty locker room and began undressing. Before they headed to the shower room, Alex gave Brandon his phone number and promised he could call him at any time if Brandon faced any problems with his parents. He was sure Liam's parents would be more than happy to put him up for a couple of nights if things went terribly wrong.

"Thanks for the number," Brandon said when they entered the shower room.

"That's so cute," Roy said with a mocking tone. "The coach is away one day, and you already have a new boyfriend."

"Did you tell them?" Brandon said to Alex. His voice raised an octave. "But you promised me," he whispered, looking at the floor.

Brandon's face was so mortified that Alex had a hard time deciding what to do. He had to say something since everybody in the room was looking at them. Most of the boys looked confused, but Roy and Kevin didn't even try to hide the smirks on their faces.

"No. We're not dating, which should be quite obvious," Alex said to Roy before he turned to look at Brandon. "I haven't told anybody anything," he said to him.

Understanding what he had just done, Brandon blushed and rushed back to the locker room. Alex wasn't sure if he should follow him there. Before he had made up his mind, Luke offered to help.

"I'll go and talk to him," he said.

"Thanks," Alex said, feeling helpless in the situation.

Alex stepped under the spigot and let the hot water massage his back. Unlike the other times, it didn't make him feel relaxed. Roy and Kevin glaring at him didn't help either.

"Should you go and comfort your boyfriend?" Roy said.

I should, but he's not my boyfriend, Alex thought. He swallowed his pride and returned to the locker room, where he found Luke talking with Brandon.

"I'm so sorry," Brandon said as soon as he saw Alex entering the room. "It was a terrible misunderstanding."

"You've nothing to apologize for," Alex said. If someone had, it was definitely Roy. "Are you okay?"

"I guess so," Brandon said. He had a sad smile on his face.

"Um, is there anything I can do about…?" Alex began, but his words trailed off as he looked at Luke.

"He already told me," Luke said.

"If the others aren't totally dumb, they should know by now that … I'm … gay," Brandon said.

"And they don't care," Luke said with such determination that it made Brandon's smile look a bit less sad.

Before Alex had a chance to say anything, some of the boys returned from the shower. Brandon hid behind Alex, unable to look them in the eyes. To his relief, none of them commented on what he had said in the shower room. Instead, they wanted to know if he was okay.

By the time everybody had returned to the locker room, Brandon had calmed down. He was still sitting on the bench, a towel wrapped around his waist.

"The shower room is empty. The faggots can go in now," Roy said.

"Roy!" Alex shouted and glared at the jock.

"Brandon, let's go and take a shower," Luke said. "I hope the rest of you will join us now that the idiots have left the shower."

Except Roy and Kevin, the whole team, even those who had already dressed, took off their clothes and followed Luke to the showers. Alex watched in amazement, and his satisfaction only increased when he saw Roy's grumpy face.

"You're no longer welcome at this camp. As soon as the coach arrives on Monday morning, I'll talk to him," Alex said to Roy. He was sure Coach Hanson would approve his decision.

"Not so fast, gay boy," Roy said.

He took his phone from the pocket of his jeans and showed Alex the picture where he was hugging Brandon in the lobby. Had Alex not been there and known why they were hugging, he might have mistaken what was happening in the picture.

He saw us, but he can't possibly think we are dating or something, Alex thought.

"There's nothing between Brandon—" Alex said, but Roy interrupted him.

"If you show your ugly face here on Monday, I'll send this picture to all the parents," Roy said. "They will be so excited to hear there is a pedophile at swim camp."

"You can't ... but that's a—" Alex began to say.

"Bye-bye, gay boy," Roy said and walked out of the locker room with Kevin.

Chapter 10

Thank God he's finally here, Liam thought when he saw Alex parking his Mustang in front of the house. The kiss in the tent was still bothering him even though he had pushed Matthew away as soon as he had realized what had happened.

Matthew had explained that his weird behavior was because of the pill he had had to take to avoid severe withdrawal symptoms. Liam wanted to believe his friend was still committed to the rehab. At least, he had been promising him the whole two-hour walk to the parking area, apart from the time he spent reassuring Liam that he was not interested in him, or men in general.

Liam didn't want to think on the car ride to Fairmont. His mother had been busy asking how their camping trip had gone, and he had been equally busy explaining how fantastic it had been.

Alex opened the door and stepped into the hall. He put his bag down on the floor and wiped sweat from his forehead. The tired look on his beautiful face turned into a cute smile when he saw Liam approaching him.

"How was your week, honey?" Liam asked and rushed to hug his boyfriend.

"Huh? It was … interesting. I'll tell you later," Alex said. "I missed you so much."

They kissed and held each other for a long time until Alex finally let go and asked if Matthew was still there. Liam led him to his room, where Matthew was lying on the bed. An uncomfortable feeling went through his body when he realized it was Alex's bed.

Matthew stood up quickly and offered his hand to Alex. "Nice to meet you. I was Liam's friend when we lived in Minnesota."

"I remember my boyfriend mentioning you," Alex said. After he had shaken hands with Matthew, he put his arm around Liam's waist.

Was it just my imagination, or did he emphasize the word "boyfriend"? Liam hoped Alex wouldn't feel jealous. At least he shouldn't have any reason. Or should he?

There was an awkward silence, and the three of them were just looking at each other. Liam thought hard about how he would tell Alex what had happened. Should he just say that the boy in his room was a drug addict? Or that they had swum naked and kissed in the tent? Neither of them sounded like a proper conversation starter.

"I guess I'm happy for Liam that you two have found each other," Matthew said. The words coming from his mouth sounded as awkward as his face looked.

"Thanks. I guess," Alex said.

"Please excuse me. I need to visit the toilet," Matthew said and walked past them out of the room.

Liam looked at Alex and raised his eyebrows.

"He seems okay," Alex said.

"Yeah. I spent most of my childhood with him," Liam said.

"And you'll spend the rest of your life with me," Alex said, smiling broadly as he wrapped his arms around Liam.

"I will," Liam said and rested his head against Alex's muscular chest.

Alex's hands rubbing and squeezing his butt increased his body's hunger. All that touching led to the inevitable. Liam began to get hard, which only encouraged Alex to continue. Soon, Alex's hand was inside Liam's boxer briefs.

"I can see that you've been missing me," Alex whispered in his ear.

Liam groaned as Alex kept fondling his growing erection. He slipped his hands under Alex's shirt and let them wander along his back. The skin was soft and warm, which made Liam want to touch it more and more.

"Um, careful there," Liam said. Alex's playing with his penis was making it throb.

"Someone is horny today," Alex said but didn't stop.

Liam felt how the pressure was building up. He took hold of Alex's hand and pulled it out of his pants. Reluctantly, Alex's fingers left Liam's pulsing manhood.

"I can't take it anymore," Liam gasped and kissed his boyfriend.

They kissed again, and a third time, and Alex's hand was wandering back to Liam's crotch when they heard someone clearing his throat at the door. That was, of course, Matthew.

"Um, I'm sorry if I interrupted something," he said.

Liam blushed and sat on the bed to hide the bulge in his shorts, which was more than obvious. It solved one problem, but there was a more urgent thing to be sorted out. He had to tell Alex about Matthew's drug problem before Mom and Dad got home from the grocery store.

"There's something we should discuss," Liam said and turned toward his boyfriend, who had sat next to him on the bed.

"Okay," Alex said and looked concerned. "What is it?"

"It's about Matthew. He's … um … how should I say this…?" Liam hesitated.

"I use drugs, and I asked if Liam could help me get into rehab," Matthew said.

"You do what?" Alex said and stood up. "You need to leave now. I don't want you to be anywhere near my boyfriend."

"Alex, please, calm down," Liam said. "Let's talk."

Liam explained how Matthew had appeared at the front door on Monday and how his friend had told him about the drugs only at the national park. Alex wanted to know everything that had happened during the camping trip, and Liam summarized the events, leaving a few details out of the story. Now wasn't the right time to talk about the kiss.

"What did your parents say?" Alex asked.

Liam was right when he assumed Alex wouldn't like the answer. "Please let's not tell them. I'll drive him to the rehab clinic first thing on Monday morning."

Alex sighed. "Can you be off the pills until that?" he asked Matthew.

"I promise," Matthew said.

"So, we shouldn't call your parents either, right?" Alex said.

"No. They can't know that I'm here."

Matthew paced around the room, tossing short glances at Alex and Liam. His breathing was becoming heavier, and Liam prepared to block his way to the backpack. There was no way he would let his friend take more pills, mollies or whatever he called them.

Alex studied Matthew so carefully that it made Liam feel uncomfortable. *He wasn't like that when we were kids*, he reminded himself.

"Why can't your parents know you're here?" Alex asked.

"Because…," Matthew said, raising his voice although he didn't complete the sentence.

"If you expect us to help you, you need to trust us," Alex said.

"Fine," Matthew said and sat on a chair. He covered his face with his hands and rubbed his forehead. "I don't live with them," he said finally.

"But, if they knew, maybe they could help you," Liam offered.

"They disowned me when they found out that I'm … that I'm using drugs," Matthew said.

His eyes became moist, and he turned away. When he began sobbing silently, Liam wanted to comfort him, but Alex stopped him. They sat on the bed, without saying a word, and let him calm down. Finally, Matthew turned to look at them.

"I never want to see them again," he said. His eyes were red and his voice barely louder than a whisper.

"You don't have to. And we will help you," Liam said, giving Alex a meaningful look.

"We will," Alex said.

Matthew stood up and surprised Alex by hugging him. Tentatively, the jock wrapped his arm around him and patted his shoulder. After the hug, Liam saw a small smile on his confused boyfriend's face.

"Thanks, guys," Matthew said and hugged Liam, too.

Liam held his friend who felt so fragile. Both of them had walked a long path since their childhood in Grand Rapids, and now their paths had crossed. He just wished Matthew's path hadn't been so rocky.

I wonder where he's lived since leaving his home, Liam thought, but before he had a chance to ask, he felt Matthew's hand on his butt. At first, it might have been an accident, but when his fingers squeezed him, Liam knew it wasn't.

He let go of his friend, took a step back, and saw a smile on Matthew's face. Neither of them said anything. Then Liam glanced at Alex, but his boyfriend wasn't watching them.

What should I do? Liam thought just as he heard his parents open the front door.

Alex thanked Liam's mother for yet another delicious meal, and the boys returned to Liam's bedroom. The rest of the house was nearly clean, but there was still plenty of stuff in Liam's closets. The next task was to throw away anything unnecessary before the company fetched the garbage container on Monday.

"Are your parents moving? Why do they want to get rid of all this stuff?" Matthew asked.

Haven't you heard that people clean every now and then? Alex thought but kept his mouth shut.

"They just want more room for themselves when I don't live here anymore," Liam said. "Dad likes to paint. This room will become his workshop."

"There's a nice view of the forest," Alex said.

He took a pile of t-shirts from the wardrobe and went through them one by one. Based on how shabby they looked, most of them had to be old. The colors had faded after being washed over and over again. Alex couldn't understand why his boyfriend hadn't tossed them away years ago.

"I remember this," Alex said. He was holding a dark shirt with pink stripes on the sleeves. "You looked so cute in this."

He tried to kiss Liam, but his boyfriend pulled his head back. Instead, Liam took the shirt and folded it carefully, double checking that the material was straight and there were no wrinkles. When he was ready, he let his gaze linger on the shirt.

"Let's put it here," Liam said and stored the shirt in a box they would take to Eddington. "The rest of them, I don't need."

"Um, do you mind if I take them?" Matthew asked.

"I can take them out," Alex said. "I was going to bring this trash bag to the container."

"I mean … can I have them?" Matthew said.

Alex gave the shirts to him. Without looking at either Alex or Liam, Matthew tossed them into his backpack. Again, there was an awkward silence in the room. After losing all financial support from his parents, Alex had been tightening his belt most of the time. Apparently, things were even worse for Matthew.

Liam's sad face made Alex feel sorry for Matthew. As far as he had understood, those two boys had been very close. Now his boyfriend was a top student at a valued university. Matthew, on the other hand, was a drug addict who seemed to have severe difficulties getting his life under control.

If things had gone differently, I would be in his shoes, Alex thought. He hadn't seen his father for months but assumed the old man was still wasted and without a job in his sleazy condo.

Trying actively to forget his father, Alex crouched and began pulling Liam's old jeans from the lowest shelf. He saw the ones Liam had been wearing when he'd visited Alex's room at their old house for the first time. He remembered how skinny Liam looked in them. Unfortunately, they were too worn out for Liam and too small for Matthew.

"There is still one t-shirt," Alex said and unfolded it.

"I want to keep that," Liam said.

"But it won't fit you anymore," Alex said and stared at the shirt. Liam must have gotten it before he'd gone to high school.

"It was a gift from Matthew."

Liam and Matthew looked at each other. Alex didn't see a point in saving an old shirt, but Matthew seemed pleased that Liam didn't let him throw it away. Apparently, none of the jeans were from him, so Alex was allowed to put them in the pile of items to be discarded.

Half an hour later, they had emptied most of the wardrobe, and Liam went to toss the last garbage bag. As soon as his boyfriend couldn't hear them, Alex used the opportunity to ask Matthew a couple of things that had been bothering him.

"You said your parents kicked you out," Alex said. "Where do you live then?"

"In Memphis," Matthew replied, avoiding Alex's gaze.

"Do you have an apartment there?"

Matthew nodded.

"Roommates?"

"Why are you so interested in how I live?" Matthew snapped.

Alex wasn't taken aback by the outburst. As a matter of fact, he had expected it. Something in Matthew told him he shouldn't trust him. He was hiding something.

"Liam has gone through a lot," Alex said. "I don't want you to cause him more trouble."

"Don't you lecture me on what is good for Liam. I've known my friend much longer than you," Matthew said.

Alex stood up and moved closer to Matthew, who didn't budge. "Just so you know, I'm very protective of my boyfriend," he said.

Matthew sneered. "By all means. Just so you know, Liam and I—"

"Whew! What's going on in here?" Liam returned to the room and interrupted their heated discussion.

"Nothing," Matthew said. "Your pal just wanted to know me better."

"Sure, okay," Liam said and rolled his eyes. "Let's calm down and play something."

Matthew took the Carcassonne box from the table and opened it enthusiastically. He set the opening tile on the floor and gave the green meeples to Liam and the red ones to Alex, who wasn't equally thrilled.

"Should we explain the rules to Alex?" Matthew asked.

"I know how to play this," Alex said. "But, why do I have one token less?"

"Oh. Sorry," Matthew said and took the missing meeple from the box and gave it to Alex.

They began playing, and it didn't take long before Alex recognized a pattern. Whenever Matthew set a new tile, he did it to either help Liam or to make his game harder. As a result, Alex lost every game, and Liam won most of them.

He must realize Matthew's doing it on purpose, Alex thought when Liam was celebrating his fifth victory.

"Don't worry, Alex. We used to play this a lot," Matthew said.

"It's fine. He can comfort me when we go to bed," Alex said and smiled at Liam. From the corner of his eye, he saw a grumpy expression on Matthew's face.

They played a couple more games before Liam's mother—to Alex's great satisfaction—came and called them for dinner. He had played enough Carcassonne to last the rest of his life. What was even better, soon Liam's possessive junkie friend would be at the rehab clinic, and they could return to Eddington.

One more week at swim camp, and then it's over, Alex thought. He wanted to talk about Roy's ultimatum with Liam, but Matthew was always hanging around. Anyway, Alex had decided to return to Buonas on Monday and call Roy's bluff. He wanted to be there when the Swimming Coaches Association guys came.

"You have done such nice work in cleaning Liam's bedroom that I made some blueberry pie for dessert," Liam's mother said after they had eaten.

Alex was about to say that it was his favorite, but Matthew was quicker. "Cool. You always made that when Liam and I had a sleepover," he said.

"Speaking of sleeping, I'll make a bed for you in the living room," she said. "The guest room is so full of boxes."

"Oh. I don't want to cause you extra trouble. I can sleep on the floor in Liam's room," Matthew said. "Assuming that's okay with you," he added and looked at Liam.

"Sure. There's enough room now," Liam said.

Alex didn't miss the smirk on Matthew's face when he turned to look at his boyfriend. Did Liam really want the annoying junkie to stay the night in their bedroom? Alex said a longing goodbye to their make-out session and took a big slice of the pie.

Three more nights and then he's gone.

Chapter 11

Matthew closed the door behind him and walked along the sidewalk. He wasn't going anywhere in particular, but he just couldn't spend more time inside the house. Putting up with Liam's cocky boyfriend all day Saturday had been a major achievement.

The smile, the flawless face, and the athletic body—it wasn't hard to understand why Liam had fallen for that guy. As if seeing them together the whole day hadn't been bad enough, Matthew was sure they had kissed and made out in the bed, thinking he was sleeping. He hadn't been, but he'd certainly wished he was.

How can I ever compete with that Mr. Fucking-Perfect? Matthew thought.

It was again one of those moments when he needed encouragement, and he knew where to get it. Without hesitation, he grabbed a smiling friend from his pocket. It was soothing to know that soon, everything would be better.

The previous pill he had taken had led to him kissing Liam. It would have been perfect, except Liam's reaction had been beyond disappointing. His best friend in the entire world had rejected him. The Liam he had known would have never done such a cruel thing.

I was too long away from his life, Matthew thought, feeling helpless. His blood began boiling when he thought of the countless hours he had sat with the therapist. It had all been for nothing, and those sessions had only made him more and more distressed.

Matthew was happy that Liam hadn't told Alex about the kiss. If he had, the jock would have kicked his ass already. The guy, who acted like Liam's bodyguard, was strong enough that a physical fight with him wouldn't end well. Matthew had to think about something else.

A phone call from his sister interrupted Matthew's brainstorming. He considered his options for a while and decided to answer.

"I'm really worried about you," she said. "Please tell me where you are."

He was about to hang up, but there was something in her voice that made him hesitate.

"Mom and Dad are furious. They think you stole money from them," she said.

"I did."

"What? Why? That was all their savings."

"They kicked me out of the house," Matthew yelled at the phone. "They got exactly what they deserved."

His magnificent parents donated most of their money to the local parish. What she called their savings was hardly five-hundred dollars. If Maria thought that he had taken more, they had lied to her to make him sound like a real criminal. That had been their special skill ever since moving to Alabama.

Sneaking into the house when both of his parents had been at work had been child's play. The real difficulty had been to convince the guy he had met at the homeless shelter to drive him all the way to Russellville. The bastard had wanted half the money.

Matthew heard his mother's voice in the background. He still recognized it even though he hadn't heard it for nearly three years, ever since he'd decided to stop seeing the therapist. Her voice made him feel sick, and he ended the call.

I need another molly, he thought and swallowed a new pill. Then he sat down on the edge of the sidewalk to wait for it to kick in.

Half an hour later, Matthew returned to Liam's house. He stopped in the front yard and looked at the freshly painted walls, the cut grass, and Liam's father's new SUV. Liam had gotten everything, even parents who adored the dumb jock.

Liam walked out of the door and greeted him happily. "Did you enjoy your walk?" he asked.

"I was thinking a lot," Matthew said.

"Okay."

"First of all, I want to apologize for the kiss."

Liam looked over his shoulder. "Can we just forget it? You were on drugs, and it didn't mean anything."

Matthew disagreed about it not meaning anything but kept his mouth shut. Instead, he flashed a broad smile, which wasn't difficult due to the pills he had taken. He wanted to get rid of the pills but retain the positive spirit. The solution to achieving that was standing in front of him.

"There is something else I wanted to tell you. I want to get clean, so I tossed these," he said in a low voice and showed Liam the empty zip-lock bag.

"That's a good start," Liam said. "I'll drive you to the clinic tomorrow."

Going to rehab made Matthew anxious. He pushed his hand into the other pocket of his jeans, where he had stored his smiling friends before showing his friend the empty bag. There were only a few left.

"Um. About the rehab. Do you think you could stay in Fairmont a bit longer?" Matthew said. "It would be nice to have a familiar face around here."

Liam didn't have a chance to answer before Alex walked out of the front door and put his arm around Liam's shoulder. He kissed him on the cheek before paying any attention to Matthew.

"Are you ready to start your new life tomorrow?" he asked.

"As a Boy Scout," Matthew said.

"Maybe you'll even make new friends there," Alex said.

I can hardly wait, Matthew thought but managed to keep the fake smile on his face.

Matthew looked at Liam's face and got the answer to his question. Alex, Liam's studies at the university, and pretty much everything was more important to Liam than him. It was happening again. Liam would leave, and he would be sent to a clinic to talk with a therapist.

The mollies he had taken were fighting to keep the darkness out of his mind. Still, Matthew felt that those tiny pieces of his collapsed world he had managed to set up were crashing down again. It was like building a house of cards on a windy beach—frustrating and pointless.

It had been a chilly December night in Minneapolis eighteen months ago. He had been wandering here and there for months and was starving and cold. Then he had met those wonderful people who had taken him to the shelter and given him that steaming soup, which had been better than anything his mother had ever cooked.

There, he had also befriended molly. At first, it had been just one pill, which those people he'd thought were his friends had offered him—for free, of course. It had filled him with happiness he hadn't felt for years. It was the best therapist he had ever had. Much better than the awful man his mother had hired.

But, those smiling pills had come with a terrible price. He had spent the following summer begging on street corners to buy more chemical therapy sessions. The more he used them to escape the real world, the more unbearable the moments without the pills were. He had been an addict for weeks before he even realized it, and then it was too late. And the money he got from strangers wasn't enough to satisfy his hunger for happiness.

Stealing whatever he could find from the local stores and selling it on the black market wasn't the worst part of finding his happiness. Neither was escaping the cops along the narrow alleys of notorious neighborhoods in Memphis. The absolutely worst thing was the realization that his life was irrevocably ruined.

After the summer, when the nights had become colder and colder, he had returned to the shelter. For a moment, everything had started to look better. But then, on a Friday afternoon a week ago, the volunteers working at the homeless shelter had found his pills and asked him to leave.

Now, Matthew needed his friend to get back on his feet. "You can't stay here for the summer?" he asked Liam.

"Here? Why?" Alex asked. "No. We'll head back to Eddington on Saturday."

"Alex is right. I'm sorry," Liam said, unable to look him in the eyes. "But I'll make sure you get proper treatment before we go."

Proper treatment. Those were his mother's exact words when she had driven him to see the therapist for the first time.

"I understand," Matthew said. On some level, he did, even though it felt unfair. The dumb jock had taken his place in Liam's life.

"After you're clean from drugs, you can come visit us in Eddington," Liam offered. "Or we can come to Memphis."

A few hours later, Matthew sat on the mattress in Liam's bedroom. Since Mr. Green had left for the airport to catch a flight to Toronto, his friend had gone to help his mother with groceries. He and Alex were alone in the house, and the jock didn't want to spend time in the same room with him, which was more than fine.

Matthew's hand was in his pocket, and his finger fumbled for his smiling friends. He knew he shouldn't, but the temptation to swallow just one more pill was getting stronger and stronger.

This is the last one, he thought—knowing it was a lie— and put the pill in his mouth. He had hardly swallowed it when Alex scared the shit out of him.

"Once a junkie, always a junkie," Alex said and cast a contemptuous glance at Matthew.

"It was just a painkiller," Matthew said.

"Even you don't believe that."

"I swear it's the truth."

Alex approached him, and Matthew was worried that if the jock found the pills, he would send him away. Liam wasn't there to defend him—and, to be honest, he wasn't even sure if Liam would defend him. Alex's hands approached the pockets of his jeans.

"Don't touch me!" Matthew yelled, shoving Alex away.

"Are you afraid of a gay guy touching you?" Alex said in a mocking tone.

"No," Matthew said. "Actually … when we were camping, Liam even kissed me."

He regretted it immediately, but at least Alex lost interest in his pills. For a moment, the jock just stared at him with a thunderstruck expression on his face.

"You're lying," he said.

"Ask Liam and ask him why he didn't tell you."

Alex stormed out of the room, but Matthew knew his problem hadn't disappeared.

Matthew woke up on Monday morning and, to his great satisfaction, noticed that Liam was sleeping alone in the bed. He sat on Alex's side of the bed and touched his friend's shoulder. The skin was warm and soft, and he wanted to let his hand wander on Liam's back.

"I hardly slept last night," he said as soon as Liam opened his eyes. "I'm so sorry I told him."

"Why did you do it?" Liam asked and glared at him with his sleepy eyes.

If Matthew had managed to cause friction between Alex and Liam, the disclosure hadn't helped his situation. In addition to their mutual quarrel, neither of them had spoken to him the previous night.

Scratching his back, Matthew tried to come up with an explanation that would sound reasonable. There was still one option, which he hadn't tried: honesty.

He paused for a long moment before saying, "I guess I was jealous."

"Of what?"

"You and Alex."

He had to admit it sounded like he had tried to sabotage their relationship on purpose. Technically speaking, that was the truth, but he should have known it required much more than just one stupid lie.

"I don't understand," Liam said. His voice was softer now.

Matthew's body tensed, and his breathing became short. With his right hand, he took hold of his left wrist to make his arms stop moving. Feeling the beat of his heart, he raised his gaze and looked Liam straight in the eyes.

"Liam, I'm gay," he said.

"So, you didn't kiss me because you were high."

Seeing the friendly and understanding expression on Liam's face ignited a small spark of hope in Matthew's heart. Maybe Liam still liked him. At least he had admitted having a crush on him.

"I love you," he said. "I always have," he added.

Liam was quiet, and Matthew studied his face, holding his breath. The only thing Liam had to say was that he loved him, too, and everything would change back to the way things were supposed to be. They could start from where they had left off on that horrible day in Grand Rapids. But, Liam didn't say what he so desperately wanted to hear.

"You were my best friend," he started, and then it came, "but you need to understand that I'm with Alex. I love him."

Liam's words closed a chapter in Matthew's life. What had started nearly twenty years ago in the forests and fields of Grand Rapids came to an end. Liam got his happy ending, and Matthew sat on the bed and stared at the wall as his fragile heart broke, piece by piece.

While Matthew was gathering his thoughts, Liam dressed in his shirt and college pants. Then he opened the curtains and let the sunlight fill the bedroom. Even the beautiful summer day couldn't improve Matthew's mood. Maybe a molly would have taken part of his pain.

"You said I was your best friend," Matthew said tentatively. "Can we still be friends?"

Liam looked at him, and his face grew severe. "We can, but you need to get clean from the drugs first."

He's making me choose between him and the pills, Matthew thought but realized that it wasn't an unreasonable condition for their friendship. Liam wanted what was best for him. He just hoped things could have been simpler.

"I'll find the address of the rehab center," Liam said and switched on his laptop.

Matthew watched Liam holding the MacBook on his lap and typing on the keyboard. He had once had a similar laptop, a stolen one, but he had sold it to buy drugs.

"Damn," Liam said and squinted his eyes. "It's closed today. We need to wait until tomorrow."

Maybe there is a god, after all, Matthew thought, relieved. "What a shame," he said.

"Don't worry. We'll get you back on your feet," Liam said and flashed a small smile.

"Thanks," Matthew said, and this time it was almost honest. He opened his arms to hug his friend, but Liam stepped back.

"I need to talk to Alex before he leaves," he said and left the room.

When Matthew arrived in the kitchen a few minutes later, the two lovebirds were hugging each other there. Alex gave him an angry glance before kissing Liam, who tightened the hold of his arms around the jock.

That show is for me, Matthew thought. He would have never believed that his friend could be so sordid.

Alex was about to say something when Mrs. Green rushed into the kitchen wearing a bathrobe and a towel wrapped around her wet hair. She greeted the boys and poured herself a big mug of coffee.

"I'm visiting my sister after work. Promised to help with the wedding preparations," she said to Liam.

"But, isn't it in August?" Liam said.

"You know Sydney. She wants to be prepared," she said and rolled her eyes. "Anyway, I'll be home very late, and your father is in Toronto the whole week. Will you be okay?"

"Mom, I'm a big boy. I think I'll survive one day without you."

"I can take care of him," Matthew offered. From the corner of his eye, he noticed that Alex didn't look particularly happy—not that it had been his purpose to please the dumb jock.

"Oh. I thought you were heading home today," she said.

"Um, there are some ... challenges with the bus connections," Liam said. "I'll drive him to the bus terminal tomorrow."

"Don't trust public transit. Besides the schedules, you never know what kind of bums and drug addicts you're traveling with," she said and left for his bedroom to get dressed.

"Yeah. You never know," Alex said with a smirk on his face.

He who laughs last, laughs best, Matthew thought. He realized both of Liam's parents would be away and the cocky jock would be out of sight, too. There were still enough mollies in his pocket to put his plan into practice. This time, Liam wouldn't stop him kissing or hugging.

In Matthew's mind, they were meant to be together. Best friends forever.

Chapter 12

Liam's mother was finishing a call with someone when Alex walked out the door with his sports bag full of clothes for the second week at camp. She thanked the caller for contacting her after such a long time and apologized that she wouldn't be home that evening.

"It was Matthew's mother," she said to Alex with a confused look on her face.

"Is she coming here?" Alex asked.

"She and his father are coming to pick up Matthew. I just can't understand why they would drive such a long way, but they seemed to be on their way already."

Why are they coming if they disowned their son? And how do they even know that he's here? Alex wondered. To be honest, anything related to Matthew shouldn't surprise him anymore. Besides, it was good if his parents took care of him instead of his boyfriend. The less time Liam spent with the junkie, the better.

"I'm glad I promised to help Sydney today," she said and grinned. Then she continued whispering, "Don't tell Liam, but I never liked that awful lady."

Alex laughed. "My lips are sealed."

"But, could you tell the boys that Matthew's parents are coming? I need to rush so I won't be late for work," she said and opened the door of her car.

Alex nodded and wished her a great day at work. He put the sports bag in the trunk of his Mustang and thought about what he should do. It was evident that Matthew didn't want to see his parents. If he kept his mouth shut, the junkie would get an unpleasant surprise. And what was best, maybe his parents would take their son with them.

The guy was asking for trouble, and Alex didn't like it at all that his boyfriend would spend the whole day alone with Matthew. He didn't want to think what stupid ideas Matthew could come up with if he knew his parents were coming for a visit.

It's best that I don't say anything, Alex thought. He waved his hand to Mrs. Green and went inside the house, where he found Liam and Matthew eating breakfast.

"Did you forget something?" Liam asked.

"No," Alex said. *I just came inside so your mother would believe I told you about Matthew's parents.*

"He probably came to check that I'm not using drugs," Matthew said. He opened his mouth and showed his empty hands.

Alex ignored him. "I just wanted to kiss you one more time before I leave," he said to Liam.

Liam's eyes were brown and friendly, and his lips were so smooth that Alex could have spent the whole morning just watching Liam's beautiful face and kissing him.

Alex was embarrassed he had gotten so angry at his boyfriend after hearing he and Matthew had kissed. He should have known Liam would never do something like that. It was only in the morning when he had calmed down enough to listen to what Liam had to say. The junkie had been so intoxicated that he would have kissed a lamp-post had there been one in the forest.

"Good luck with the headhunters," Liam said and kissed him one more time. "Show them what a kick-ass coach you are."

Unless Coach Hanson kicks my ass first, Alex thought while he was walking to his car.

Roy had repeated his threat on Sunday evening, as if Alex's day hadn't been bad enough because of the argument with Liam. The asshole had sent the picture of him and Brandon hugging together with a text: "Happy to not see you on Monday."

He had already decided, several times, that he wouldn't let the jock get under his skin. Even if Roy had the guts to send the picture to the parents of the kids on the swim team, which Alex doubted, Coach Hanson wasn't a homophobe. The coach would support him for sure. Still, Alex found it hard to turn the key to start the engine of his Mustang.

Is this really worth all this? Alex asked himself and squeezed the steering wheel.

He didn't have to think for long when he knew the answer. Yes, he wanted nothing more than to see Roy's cocky face when the jock realized he wasn't afraid of him or his empty threats.

Alex started the car and drove along Maple Street toward the highway to Buonas. He didn't notice Liam looking out the window and waving at him. And he especially didn't notice the triumphant smirk Matthew had on his face as he stood behind Liam.

"Good morning," Alex said to the boys who were changing their clothes in the locker room.

"Hi. What's up?" Luke greeted him enthusiastically.

Alex scanned the room and noticed everybody had arrived. Roy scowled at him, but Alex ignored it. The jock had a lot to learn if he wanted to build up a professional athletic career. It was as much attitude as it was muscles.

"Roy, since you're ready, come and help me get the kickboards from the closet. The rest of you, we'll meet at the pool in five," Alex said and left the room.

The jock muttered something but followed him to the equipment storage. Alex switched on the lights to the small room and the opened locker.

"We'll practice kick technique today," he said. "Please take ten of those blue kickboards."

Roy bent over to reach the boards that were piled on the floor. Alex amused himself with the idea of slapping the jock on his butt. Of course, he didn't, but when Roy turned around, Alex had a broad smile on his face.

"What's so funny?" Roy asked.

"Beautiful morning," Alex said.

"Enjoy it as long as you can. I'll send the picture tonight."

"No, you won't."

Alex managed to keep his poker face. Lately, the media had been full of news about assaults and sexual harassment in Hollywood. Any news agency would be eager to publish a story about a swim coach molesting minors at a training camp, even though it was not true. Alex had to play his cards right.

"We both know I was just comforting Brandon," he said.

"Why would he need any comfort from you?"

"None of your business. Just remember that spreading false accusations is a felony. You're still young. You can hate me if you want, but don't let it ruin your life."

Roy gave him a suspicious look but left the room without another word. Alex congratulated himself on how he had handled the situation. He locked the storage room and headed to the pool where the boys were already waiting for him.

"You five, take the first lane. The rest of you, swim in the second lane," Alex began. "Take your boards, and let's start the drill."

They had practiced over an hour before Coach Hanson appeared at the pool area. He wanted to meet the whole team at the auditorium in half an hour, so

Alex asked the boys to hit the showers. Roy looked at him as he had expected Alex to have a task for him again, but Alex began collecting the kickboards.

"I can help with them," Brandon offered.

"Sure, thanks," Alex said, but he couldn't help noticing the meaningful look on Roy's face.

"I told my parents," Brandon said when they were alone.

"You did? How did it go?" Alex asked.

"Mom said she already knew," Brandon said and blushed lightly. "But, they were so supportive and proud of me."

Alex was happy for Brandon and wished his parents had been as cool. One day, he would face his father and settle things once and for all. That day, however, wasn't soon.

"So, do you have a boyfriend?" Alex asked.

The red color on Brandon's face deepened. He shook his head shyly, which made Alex smile. Based on their discussion the previous week, he could tell Brandon was a smart guy. For sure, there would be plenty of boys who would like to date him.

They'd hardly made it back to the locker room before Roy got his next opportunity to demonstrate the less attractive side of his character.

"Did you get your next date set?" he said.

Alex sighed and scowled at him but decided to say nothing.

"What? Why won't you tell us?" Kevin accompanied his friend.

"If you really need to know," Brandon said, raising his voice. "I told Alex that I came out to my parents on Saturday."

For a moment, there was complete silence in the locker room. Roy and Kevin looked at each other, and neither of them seemed to be sure what to say next. Then Luke, who had just arrived from the shower and was towel-drying his hair, tossed the towel on the bench and walked to Brandon.

"I'm so proud of you," he said and wrapped his arms around the boy, squeezing him tight against his bare chest.

Brandon seemed to have a hard time deciding where to put his hands as he hadn't expected his naked teammate to hug him. Finally, he touched Luke's back with his right hand.

"Is everything okay now?" Luke asked after he had released Brandon.

"Yeah … I guess," Brandon said and looked down. "I hope you don't mind me being…."

"Gay, straight. Who cares?" Luke said and gave Roy and Kevin a glance.

The two jocks didn't look too enthusiastic, but the other boys in the locker room seemed to agree with Luke. They assured Brandon he was still welcome to the team, and many of them patted his shoulder. All the attention made Brandon seemingly abashed, but a small smile appeared on his face.

"If you have a crush on him, too, none of my business," Roy said to Luke.

"That's where we agree. It definitely isn't your business," Luke said.

Roy didn't argue with Luke. Instead, he put on his jeans and left with Kevin. Once they were gone, the discussion turned to the swimming competition the following day.

Alex waited in the locker room until everybody had washed and dressed up. Even though the boys had taken the news well, he didn't want anybody to cause any trouble for Brandon on his watch.

Soon, they had all gathered in the auditorium. Coach Hanson was standing on the podium and rubbing his belly while he calculated that everybody was present.

"There have been some challenges in arranging the swimming competition," he started. "The primary timing system is under maintenance, and the weather forecast doesn't look too good, considering there are only outdoor pools here."

The auditorium went silent, and the boys had severe looks on their faces. Alex understood their disappointment. The competition had always been one of the highlights of the camp.

"However, I have some good news," the coach continued. "I agreed with the other schools that we will have the competition in Fairmont on Wednesday."

"In our high school swim hall?" someone asked.

"We'll go there tomorrow. First, we'll practice, and then in the afternoon, we'll prepare everything for the competition," Coach Hanson explained.

There was some confusion in the room. Not all the boys were happy that the camp was interrupted and everybody had to return home today. On the other hand, they still got the competition they had expected.

"And, as you know, there will be two swimmers representing our team," Coach Hanson continued. "Alex will now come up here to announce whom he has chosen."

"Shit. That can't be true," Alex heard Roy muttering behind him.

Maybe not those exact words, but that could have been Alex's reaction as well. The coach had asked for his recommendation, but he'd had no idea he would make him decide, unprepared and in front of the team.

Alex stood up and walked to the podium. Roy stared at him, and Alex saw anger, disappointment, and frustration in his eyes. With his athletic merits, Roy deserved the place in the competition, but this would be a perfect opportunity for revenge. One name from his mouth, and Roy would be out of the game.

Liam would never make it personal, Alex thought and touched his engagement necklace through his shirt.

"Swimming, like any sport, is not just muscles, power, and winning," Alex said. "We are idols for some, heroes for many, and we should carry that role with respect and humbleness, letting our actions reflect our values."

He had no idea where those words were coming from, but everybody in the room, even Coach Hanson, was listening to him in total silence. He moved on in his speech as everybody was waiting for his decision.

"I have made up my mind," Alex said before pausing to consider one more time whether he had made the right decision. "The Fairmont High School participants for the competition are Luke and … Roy."

The announcement surprised nobody except Roy. The jock had a confused look on his face as he stared at Alex. He didn't even notice Luke, who offered his hand to congratulate his teammate. Only when Luke poked his shoulder did a satisfied smile appear on his face.

Alex nodded at the boys whom he had just selected for the competition and returned to his seat in the front row. Coach Hanson took his place at the podium and watched Alex with a fatherly look on his face.

"There will be scouts from some colleges following the practice tomorrow," he said and got the attention of the excited audience immediately. "Also, the Swimming Coaches Association guys from Eddington will be there to recruit our talented assistant coach."

Suddenly, Alex realized he hadn't thanked Liam for arranging this opportunity. His boyfriend was such a sweetheart, but the freak he had found in Liam's bedroom had taken all his attention.

Thank God he'll be gone tomorrow, Alex thought.

The competition being at Fairmont also meant Alex could spend the next two nights with Liam. That was a very welcomed bonus. Things couldn't have been better until he walked into Roy at the corridor after the lecture.

"I know why you chose me for the team," Roy said.

"You're a good swimmer," Alex said and was about to continue on his way to the cafeteria, but Roy stopped him.

"If you think you can buy my silence, you're wrong."

"What do you mean?"

"I'll show the photo to the association guys," Roy said venomously. "Good luck getting any coaching job," he added and left for lunch.

Alex stared at his back, speechless. *What an ungrateful asshole*, he thought but decided not to change the swimmers in the competition. Besides, it was probably too late anyway.

Coach Hanson joined him, and they walked to the cafeteria. The chicken, pasta, and vegetables would have been his favorite, but Alex wasn't hungry. All he could think about was whether Roy would put his threat into practice—and, if he did, what that would mean to his job as an assistant coach.

There was a reason for the hug in the picture. Alex could explain it if he were given a fair chance. Would they listen to him? Would they understand? Alex couldn't remember Coach Hanson hugging anyone at practice.

Am I just overthinking all this? Alex asked himself and realized that the coach was talking to him.

"Huh? Sorry. What did you say?" Alex asked.

"Just that you chose the right kids for the competition," the coach said, his mouth full of chicken and pasta.

"They have the best chance against the other schools."

"I'll let you take care of the practice tomorrow. The association people will see you in action."

Alex thanked the coach, even though it was his most absent-minded comment in the discussion. He wasn't anymore sure if it really mattered how he performed in the practice.

"Is something bothering you?" the coach asked, giving him a perfect opportunity to get help with the problem.

"No. I guess I'm just tired," Alex replied.

"I should call Liam and ask him to let you sleep," the coach said and laughed.

Alex forced a smile on his face.

Alex stared at the phone so intently that he didn't notice Roy, who was climbing out from the pool. At the last minute, he stepped aside, but their shoulders hit each other.

"Fuck!" Roy shouted so loud that the walls of the buildings echoed his curse.

"Roy! Watch your mouth," Coach Hanson yelled from the other side of the pool. He had just arrived to tell the team that the boys could go home as soon as they finished practice.

"Sorry, Coach. I just hit my toe against the railing," Roy said and gave Alex an angry glance.

"Guys, hit the showers," the coach ordered. "And Roy, you'll collect all the equipment and take it to the locker."

Roy began to detach the backstroke ledges from the pool. Alex wanted to help him; after all, it was partly his fault that the coach had given him the job. He just wasn't sure if the jock would appreciate his help.

"Could you please lock the doors after everybody has left? I'm a bit busy," Coach Hanson said to Alex and walked inside the building.

By the time Roy had taken the ledges to the closet, Alex had collected the kickboards. Not that Alex had expected it, but no kudos was given when the jock snatched them from Alex's hands and carried them to the storage closet.

Alex fetched his bag from the locker room and moved out of the building to wait for Roy to take a shower and get dressed. It wasn't long before the jock stormed to his car without saying a word. He started the engine and pressed the gas pedal.

The black SUV approached Alex along the narrow road from the parking area to the main gate. When the car reached the place where Alex was standing near the main building, Roy turned to look at him, showing his middle finger from the window.

Wow. That was innovative, Alex thought and turned to walk toward his car when he heard a sound of heavy braking.

Despite his effort to steer right, Roy's SUV slid from the road into a big flowerbed. He tried to back up, but the tires sank deep into the soft ground. The car was firmly stuck, and the furious driver jumped out of it and cursed loudly.

Alex dropped his sports bag and jogged to the car. "Let me push from the front. Maybe we can get it out," he said.

Roy muttered something but returned to the front seat and started the engine. From the first attempt, it was clear the car was way too heavy. Alex looked around, but he and Roy were the only ones left.

"Let's leave it there," he said. "I can drive you to Fairmont."

There was a massive amount of hesitation on Roy's face. "Thanks," he said finally but still looked away.

The jock followed Alex to his car. They didn't speak to each other, even though Alex had the awkward feeling that he should say something. He just couldn't figure out what it could be. He opened the trunk, and they put their bags inside.

"I can bring a rope with me on Thursday," Alex said when they sat in the front seats. "Unless you come to get it with your parents earlier," he added.

"Okay," Roy said and rubbed his thighs.

Alex drove his Mustang to the highway. It was early Monday afternoon, and there were only a few other cars. Most of the time, it was just the two of them and the awkward silence in the car.

They had driven half an hour when Roy asked if Alex could pull off the road. He had to take a leak. Alex found a place where he could stop the car by the side of the road. He turned his head in the other direction and waited until Roy returned to the car.

"You've got a nice car," Roy said.

"I got it from my parents when I turned sixteen," Alex said.

Roy was silent for a moment. Then he asked, "Why are you helping me?"

"Should I have left you there instead?"

Maybe Roy would have deserved that. Still, as an associate coach, Alex was responsible for the team—and, needless to say, abandoning the jock there wouldn't have been the right thing to do.

"You're a talented athlete," Alex said.

"Okay."

"I had a friend. You remind me of him."

Roy stared at the hills on the horizon. It would still take almost an hour before they were in Fairmont. He tilted the backrest and took a better position on the seat.

"Was he a swimmer, too?" he asked.

"Yup. Although, he's in prison now."

"Did he shoot you hugging other boys, too?"

"We were cool until he tried to kill my boyfriend."

They came to a small suburb, and Alex stopped the car at a traffic light. He switched to the left lane so he could bypass the black Fairmont Express truck, which was in front of them. Soon, the light turned to green.

"You're about to start your senior year, right? Do you have any plans after high school?" Alex asked.

"Look. I appreciate that you're helping me, but we don't have to pretend we're friends," Roy said and breathed hard.

Friends don't blackmail each other, Alex thought. "As you wish," he said and switched on the radio.

Soon, he had to turn it off as his phone began ringing. It was Liam's mother, who wanted to know if Alex had heard anything about Liam. She had tried to call her son the whole morning without success.

"I'm actually on my way there. The swimming competition was moved to Fairmont. I'll ask Liam to call you," Alex said.

Goddamn Matthew. If you've done something…, Alex thought and chose Liam's number on his phone. Liam didn't answer him either.

"Wow. What happened?" Roy asked when Alex suddenly accelerated.

Alex stared at the road and squeezed the steering wheel. *Matthew happened.*

Chapter 13

Behind Liam's back, Matthew watched as the red Mustang backed down the driveway. The dumb jock had left the house. The smile on Matthew's face grew broader. They were finally alone, just like he had wished.

Matthew wanted to run his finger along Liam's back, hold his narrow waist, and touch his butt before pulling his jeans down to continue the investigation. He didn't. This time, he wouldn't let his impatience screw things up.

He stepped closer to Liam. When Liam had stopped waving at Alex and moved away from the window, their bodies touched. The contact was brief, but it aroused him. He took hold of Liam's shoulder to prevent him from falling.

"Oh. Sorry," Liam said.

"No. It was my fault," Matthew said. "Just wanted to see him leaving. Cool car."

"Since when have you been interested in cars?"

Since they started taking my problems away, Matthew thought and laughed at Liam's comment.

It was true that, in their childhood, they had spent more time wandering in the forest and cycling along the gravel roads than watching how older guys fixed their cars. Matthew doubted it was only because neither of them had an older brother. Cars just hadn't been their thing.

"It's your last day here. What would you like to do?" Liam asked.

You have no idea, Matthew thought. Before he managed to say anything, Liam proposed they go out and walk to the park to enjoy the sun.

"Um … would you mind if we stayed here and played something?" Matthew said.

"I just thought, since it's such nice weather," Liam said and looked disappointed.

"Hmm. I guess you're right," Matthew admitted and looked at the clock on the wall. "Maybe a short walk and then we can play, okay?"

They walked along the street, which was surrounded by houses. It was a peaceful neighborhood filled with happy families. Matthew didn't see abandoned houses, dark corners, or small alleys where people like him used to meet after midnight to buy drugs from the rude dealer who smelled dirty and was always late.

They hadn't walked far when Liam stopped to talk to an older lady who seemed to be annoyingly interested in his studies. Matthew continued walking and stopped at the next crossing. When he turned around, Liam was still listening to what she had to say.

We should keep going so we have enough time before his mother comes back, Matthew thought. He tried to give Liam a meaningful look, but his friend didn't notice it.

Instinctively, Matthew pushed his hand into the pocket of his jeans. He counted the number of mollies and decided he could take one. The rest of the pills he would save for Liam.

They'll get him to love me again. They'll make everything be the way it should be, Matthew thought and swallowed the pill.

The euphoria the molly gave him helped Matthew to stand the endless walk around the town. Still, he was restless, and all he could think of was Liam's cute face, his slender body, the delicate arms that swayed when he walked, and his firm but squeezable butt. Everything about Liam was so perfect that Matthew wanted to wrap his arms around him and never let go.

"There was a circus here a couple of years ago," Liam said and pointed to a big empty area next to the park.

"Did Alex work there as a clown?" Matthew asked and chuckled.

Liam gave him an odd look.

"Just kidding," Matthew said and patted Liam on his shoulder. He let his hand linger there for a moment before he reluctantly pulled his arm back.

"Do you remember the big circus in Minneapolis?" Liam asked.

"How could I forget?" Matthew said. "You wanted to see it every summer."

"I thought you liked it, too."

How couldn't he have liked it? They always went there with Liam's parents, and they usually spent the weekend in a hotel where he shared a room with his best friend. The more he thought about it, the more he missed their childhood in Grand Rapids.

"Liam," Matthew said and waited until his friend turned to look at him. "I'm … I'm really happy I met you again, even though—"

"Me, too," Liam interrupted him. "And you will get your life in order. Trust me."

But I don't want any fucking therapy. I want you! You're my rehab, a voice inside Matthew's head screamed. Why didn't his friend understand that the solution to all his problems was standing there straight in front of him?

They walked through the gates to a park, which Liam so eagerly wanted to show him. To Matthew's disappointment, there were many people sitting on the grass and enjoying the sun.

"Is this place okay?" Liam asked.

Matthew didn't want to waste more time wandering around the park. He sat down in the shadow of a big tree. It was a warm day, and the pill made him sweat more than usual—but that wasn't the only impact the drug had on him. When Liam sat close to him, Matthew began to get aroused.

I need to wait until we get back to his house. The more he thought about what they would do as soon as they were alone, the harder his erection grew in his boxers. Actually, the boxers were Liam's.

"Wait here. I'll get us something to drink," Matthew said.

The girl pulling the sales trolley had appeared at the perfect moment. He needed some distraction, or he would make a move that would ruin his entire plan. He stood up and adjusted his crotch quickly. When he put his hand in his pocket and felt the pills, a wicked smile appeared on his face.

Of course. Why didn't I think of this sooner? he thought and rushed toward the girl before she got too far.

Matthew got two soda bottles, and after he had paid for them, he kneeled as if he were tying the laces of his sneakers. He opened one of the sodas and crushed one of his smiling friends, carefully dropping the crumbs inside the pop. They hissed ominously as they dissolved, and Matthew screwed the lid back on tight.

I hope he doesn't taste it, Matthew thought when he returned to Liam with the drinks.

"Thanks," Liam said and took a big gulp. "I didn't realize how thirsty I was."

Matthew followed carefully how Liam took two more sips from the bottle. The first part of the plan was successfully completed. Now he would just wait.

Two hours later, they were back at Liam's house. Liam was taking off his t-shirt, and Matthew's eyes were glued to his naked chest. He was beautiful, absolutely gorgeous.

"Jeez, I'm sweating," Liam giggled. "But it was fun, wasn't it? Please tell me that you enjoyed the walk to the park."

Liam got the shirt off, but he had to take hold of the wall to keep from falling down. Matthew moved closer in case he had to steady his friend.

"Why is the room rocking? Is it an earthquake?" Liam asked.

"Maybe. I felt something, too," Matthew said.

Giggling, Liam went to the bathroom.

Matthew noticed Liam's phone on the desk. He was studying it when it began ringing. Of course, it was Alex; who else could it have been? Matthew declined the call quickly and switched off the phone. He stormed to the kitchen and opened the freezer. Nobody would find the phone there.

Have a nice day, dumb jock.

When Liam came back from the bathroom, his face was pale. He took hold of the walls and furniture to keep balance. Apparently, the dose had been too strong for someone who wasn't used to mollies.

"I'm not feeling well," Liam said.

"Maybe you're dehydrated. It's a warm day," Matthew said. "Let me get you something to drink."

He took a bottle of Coke from the fridge and poured Liam a big glass. This time, he didn't add any extra flavor from his pocket. That had been his original plan, but Liam's condition indicated he would have to wait. Luckily, time was on his side.

Liam tried to hold the glass in his shaky hands but poured half of the drink on his naked chest.

"Let me help," Matthew offered as he took the glass from Liam and put it on the desk.

He found paper towels near the sink and began to wipe Liam's belly. Liam's shorts were soaked, too, and Matthew couldn't resist rubbing his friend's crotch with the paper. Luckily, Liam didn't resist but found it funny. His eyes were glassy, and he had a goofy smile on his face.

Matthew put the paper towels away and helped Liam to drink. They were standing close to each other, Liam leaning against him with his hand wrapped around Matthew's shoulder. Matthew used his left arm to pull his friend even closer until Liam's hip touched his swelling penis.

"Can you take me to the bed?" Liam asked.

My pleasure, Matthew thought and walked his friend to the bedroom. He set Liam onto his back on the bed and lay down next to him. Liam closed his eyes but opened them when Matthew stroked his chest with his fingers.

"What are you doing?" Liam slurred.

"Just rest. I'll take good care of you," Matthew said and moved his hand lower toward Liam's crotch.

"Please, don't," Liam said softly and closed his eyes.

Ignoring him, Matthew touched Liam's penis through his shorts. Liam moved, trying to stop him. Matthew took a better position on the bed and decided to remove Liam's shorts. He was untying the knot when Liam suddenly turned and raised his head.

Matthew closed his eyes but heard far too well how Liam vomited his breakfast on the floor. It was the worst turnoff ever.

"Could you please clean it?" Liam said and wiped his mouth on the blanket.

"Sure," Matthew sighed.

By the time he had wiped the floor, Liam was snoring quietly on his bed. He looked so small and vulnerable that Matthew decided to let him sleep. When he woke up, he would give him half a molly. Then they would finally have sex.

Chapter 14

Alex drove along Maple Street as fast as he could. He parked in front of Liam's house and stood up. Roy followed him to the front door. Alex opened the door, and they entered the hall.

"Liam! Are you here?" Alex shouted before he realized that his boyfriend was screaming.

"Help!" Liam shouted.

The voice came from his bedroom. Alex didn't understand why Liam laughed after he had first cried for help, but he wanted to find out what was going on. He rushed to the bedroom and found Liam laughing hysterically on the bed. Matthew was on top of him, kissing his neck.

"What the fuck are you doing?" Alex roared.

"Help me. He's tickling me," Liam slurred.

Alex took hold of Matthew's arm and yanked him out of the bed. Alex was about to ask Liam for an explanation when he saw his bloodshot and glassy eyes. Anger boiling in his veins, he pushed Matthew against the wall.

"What did you give him?" Alex asked.

"Please don't blame him. We were just having fun," Liam giggled.

"Help him get dressed. We need to take him to the hospital," Alex said to Roy.

Without hesitation, Roy took Liam's shirt from the floor and began dressing him. Liam grabbed Roy's crotch and snickered, but the jock moved his hand away decisively.

"I'll ask you one more time. What did you give him?" Alex said to Matthew. The tone of his voice didn't give Matthew an option to not answer.

"One of these," he said, showing Alex a pill he had taken from his pocket.

"I'll take Liam to the hospital. Can you wait here and make sure he doesn't go anywhere?" Alex said to Roy. "His parents should be here soon. They can take care of that piece of shit."

Matthew's eyes were big and full of terror. He tried to run out of the room, but Roy blocked him at the door. Matthew didn't stop but kept hitting and kicking the big jock, who rather easily got hold of his wrist and turned it behind his back.

"My parents can't find me," Matthew whined.

Liam tried to go and hug his friend, who was close to tears, but Alex stopped him. He pulled his boyfriend against his strong chest and felt how Liam's heart was beating rapidly as his body shook a bit.

"Please let me go," Matthew said. "I promise you'll never see me again."

It was a very tempting offer, and Alex was about to ask Roy to set him free when they heard the noise of a car outside. Matthew panicked and tried to free himself from Roy's strong grip.

Alex sighed. "I'll give you one chance to tell the truth," he said to Matthew. "Why shouldn't I let your parents take you?"

"My dad will beat me, and then they'll force me back into therapy," Matthew sobbed and looked Alex in the eyes. "I'm gay."

That's exactly what you deserve, Alex thought, but the scared expression on Matthew's face told him the junkie was finally telling the truth. He was a runaway, abandoned by his parents who didn't accept that he was gay. And Liam's former best friend.

"Don't make me regret this, but I'll help you," Alex said.

A teardrop rolled down Matthew's face. "Thanks," he said in a small voice.

There was the sound of a doorbell, and soon somebody stepped in. Alex realized they must have left the front door open.

"Anybody home?" a female said. Alex didn't recognize it, but based on Matthew's reaction, it had to be his mother.

Alex put his hand in front of Liam's mouth—for some reason, his boyfriend found the situation funny—and gave his car key to Roy.

"Take Matthew with you and go out of the back door," he whispered. "Quickly."

"Where should we go?" Roy asked, holding the key in his hand.

"Drive along the street and take the first street on the left. Wait for us there, okay?"

Roy nodded. He and Matthew sneaked into the corridor and opened the door of the utility room. Alex heard the back door screech and hoped he could trust Roy. Matthew, he definitely didn't trust, but the jock had behaved pretty decently the rest of the car ride.

"Is someone there?" the woman asked.

Alex heard approaching steps. He pushed Liam on the bed and lay next to him, wrapping his arms gently around the giggling boy. They began kissing just before someone entered the room.

"Liam? Is that you? Oh, dear God," the lady said and covered her mouth with her hand.

"Good evening, Mrs. Evans. So nice to see you," Liam slurred.

"I knew it!" she said, her face showing her disgust. "You made my son gay."

"That is not true," Alex said, raising his voice. "Liam didn't—"

"I didn't ask your opinion," she said. "Where's Matthew?"

Her husband walked into the room. His jaw dropped when he saw them on the bed holding each other. He looked at his wife, who gave him a meaningful look.

"Matthew was here, but he left this morning," Alex said. "So, you can leave, too."

"I'll call Mrs. Green and tell her what's going on in here," she said.

"She knows we're dating."

"Don't tell me she approves of it," Mrs. Evans said to Alex and then looked at her husband. "I always thought her moral compass was broken."

"Could you please excuse us now? I would like to fuck my boyfriend," Alex said. "Unless you want to stay and watch, of course."

Mrs. Evans fixed her jacket, muttered something, and turned around. She took hold of her husband's arm and dragged him out of the house. Liam laughed hysterically and seemed unable to stop. Alex was concerned he would choke. Finally, he was able to fill his lungs with fresh oxygen.

"Honey, how are you?" Alex asked.

Liam watched him with his glassy eyes, a broad smile on his face. "I've never felt better," he slurred.

"Come on. I'll take you to the hospital."

"But, Matthew was about to fuck me. Where is he?"

I will fucking kill that guy, Alex thought, but tried to keep his calm. "You can do that later. We need to go now," he said.

Alex knew, or at least hoped, that moment would never come. For a moment, he regretted his decision to help Matthew, but after seeing his parents, he almost felt sorry for the boy. Right now, however, the most important thing was to get Liam to the hospital.

They went to the kitchen, and Alex poured Liam a large mug of water, hoping it would help. He looked out the window and saw Matthew's parents sitting in their car. She was talking on her phone.

"They're still there. Let's use the back door," Alex said.

"I never liked that witch," Liam said.

Alex smiled and walked Liam through the utility room. It felt awful to see his boyfriend so high that he had to leave him leaning against the wall while he checked if the Evans were still there in front of the house. They were.

"We need to go through the Harlows' backyard so they don't see us," Alex whispered.

"I hope their dog isn't there," Liam said, far too loud.

"Shh! I don't want them to hear us."

"But … you just wanted to fuck me in front of them," Liam said even louder.

It wasn't Liam's fault, but the situation was getting on Alex's nerves. He put his hand on Liam's mouth and dragged him to the back of the yard where there was a small gap in the fence.

They got to the other side, and Alex pondered their options. He couldn't see anybody, but he didn't want to hold his boyfriend like he had kidnapped him. Unfortunately, Liam found it impossible to be silent, and Alex ended up walking his giggling boyfriend to the other side of the yard. Luckily, there were no more houses before the place where he hoped Roy and Matthew would be waiting for them.

"Kiss me," Liam said and looked at Alex with his glassy eyes.

I need to get him to the hospital and fast, Alex thought but fulfilled his boyfriend's wish.

"Would you have been mad if I had fucked Matthew?" Liam slurred.

Alex sighed. "We can talk about it later. Let's go walk through that grove. My car should be there."

"I need to pee first," Liam said.

Alex rolled his eyes and helped Liam to open the fly of his shorts. He had to hold him to keep him from falling. Liam found the situation unbelievably funny but managed finally to take care of his business.

"Wanna jerk me off?" Liam said.

"I do, but not now," Alex said with some urgency in his voice. He heard the sound of a car, and it sounded far too familiar.

They rushed to the other side of the grove, and as he had feared, the street was empty. The bastard had taken his car and left with the junkie.

"Fuck!" Alex cursed and glanced at Liam like it was his fault.

Chapter 15

"How could I be such an idiot to trust that jerk?" Alex thought aloud.

"Who ... who is he ... by the way?" Liam stammered.

They heard tires screeching. When Alex turned, he saw his red Mustang approaching rapidly. It stopped in front of them, leaving black marks on the road.

Roy opened the window. "Get in. Fast," he said and looked back toward the junction. The gray SUV, Matthew's parents' car, was there.

Alex pushed Liam to the backseat and ran around the car. He had hardly stepped in when Roy pressed the gas pedal, and the Mustang jumped forward. The gray SUV followed them, but the distance between the cars was increasing.

"Where the hell did you go?" Alex asked.

"We returned to the house," Roy said. "It took you so long we thought something had happened."

"Okay. Drive to the hospital as fast as you can."

"What do you think I'm doing?"

Liam's eyes were crimson, and he looked sleepy. Alex touched his hand gently, which hardly caused any reaction. Alex wrapped his arm around Liam and pulled him against his side. Liam had to stay awake until they got to the hospital.

"If something happens to him, you'll face something much worse than your parents," Alex said to Matthew.

The junkie was smart enough to stay quiet.

I need to call his mother, Alex realized and took his phone. He dialed her number, and she answered instantly.

"He did *what*?" Liam's mother yelled through the phone as soon as Alex had explained what had happened.

"He says the pills are ecstasy," Alex repeated and glared at Matthew.

"Wait for me at the hospital," she said. "And keep that boy as far as possible from my son."

"You can count on me for that."

"Alex, thank you."

They had to stop at a traffic light. Alex shook Liam to keep him awake while Roy kept glancing in the rear-view mirror. He cursed when he saw the gray SUV appearing from the side street. At the moment, Alex couldn't care less what happened to Matthew.

When the light changed, Roy speeded up. They were only a few miles from the hospital. When they got there, Matthew jumped out of the car and ran behind the buildings.

"Should I go after him?" Roy asked.

"No. Let him go," Alex said. "Help me get Liam to the ER."

They carried Liam inside the building, and Alex explained to the receptionist what had happened. Soon, two paramedics rushed over, pushing a hospital bed. An older lady in a white coat followed them.

"What has he taken?" she asked with a disapproving look on her face.

"He was given ecstasy," Alex said and gave her the pill he had gotten from Matthew. "It was crushed into his drink."

"How many?"

"I'm not sure. Maybe two."

"Has he used these before?"

"No!" Alex cried.

"I'm sorry, sir. I just need to know," she said and touched Alex on his arm.

The paramedics put Liam on the bed, pushed him through the doors, and asked Alex to wait in the lobby. Only when he sat down did he realize he hadn't even asked if Liam would be okay. Seeing his boyfriend in such a condition had been painful, but only now when he could no longer do anything did the tears begin rolling down his cheeks.

"I'm sure he'll be fine," Roy said.

Alex turned to look at him. The jock had a shy, soft smile on his face. Alex wasn't sure if he should hug him, but he decided not to. Instead, he wiped his eyes and nodded.

"I should probably drive you home," he said.

"You helped me when my car got stuck," Roy said. "It's my turn. I'll wait here with you until we hear more about your … boyfriend."

"Thanks."

"And I guess you're not as big a jerk as I thought," Roy said, punching Alex's shoulder.

It felt genuinely good to hear that. Maybe the jock wasn't such a big jerk either. At least he had helped him to get Liam to the hospital … unless this was one of his sick games again. Roy seemed sincere, though.

"Can I ask what—?" Alex began to ask when Mrs. Evans rushed into the lobby.

"Where's my son?" she asked in a loud voice.

"Not here," Alex said.

"Where is he then?"

"Ask and it will be given to you. Seek and you will find."

She snorted and scanned the room one more time. Once she was convinced that Matthew wasn't there, she marched to the front door and took hold of the handle. Before opening the door, she turned to look at Alex one more time.

"You know that you queers will burn in hell," she said and walked out of the hospital.

"I know. At least it's warm there," Alex said and got Roy to laugh at the comment.

Fifteen minutes later, it was Liam's mother's turn to rush into the lobby and ask for her son. Alex explained how the staff had taken Liam and that, so far, they hadn't told him anything. She marched to the reception desk but returned soon with the same instructions to sit and wait.

It was frustrating, but finally, the doctor came to the lobby.

Alex stood near the pools in the Fairmont High swim hall and gave instructions to the boys. Coach Hanson sat in the grandstand and followed the practice together with the Swimming Coaches Association representatives. Alex tried to ignore them and act like he had seen the coach doing when he was on the team.

He felt tired. It had been a long night at the hospital, even after the doctor had told him that Liam would be okay and they wanted to monitor him overnight. Alex had watched his boyfriend sleeping on the bed, and it had been well past midnight when Liam's mother had finally convinced him they could go home and have some sleep.

"Roy and Luke," Alex shouted. "Take the third lane and practice starts for the competition tomorrow."

The boys climbed out of the pool and walked by the stand. Roy stepped on it and adjusted his goggles. Then he took the starting position.

"Does this look good?" he asked.

"Let me check," Alex said. He raised Roy's hip a bit. "I think that is perfect."

Roy jumped into the water and swam to the midpoint before he stopped and looked back.

"Excellent!" Alex shouted and raised his thumb. "Fifteen repeats and then you can have a break."

The longer Alex spent time there coaching the boys and breathing the scent of chlorine, the more he thought it was where he belonged. It was especially nice to be back in the same hall where he had started his swimming pursuit. But, it wasn't just about sports. Suddenly, he missed all his friends from the team.

I wonder how Tristan and Colin are doing, he thought and decided to email his former teammates as soon as he got back to Eddington.

Alex's eyes grew wistful when he realized he would probably return to this hall for the last time tomorrow for the swimming competition. One chapter in his life would be closed since he knew he and Liam would never move back to Fairmont. Of course, they would visit Liam's parents as long as they lived here.

Through the big windows, Alex saw the field where he had played soccer with his friends. Behind the field was the red-brick high school building. He stared at the window of the history class and imagined Mr. Timothy talking to his students there.

Was it just a coincidence that he paired Liam and me to do that exercise? Alex thought. Either way, he owed the teacher a big thank you.

Twenty minutes later, Luke and Roy had completed their starting practices and headed toward the showers. Just before they got there, Roy turned and walked to the grandstand where Coach Hanson and his swim coach colleagues were sitting. He conversed with them for a while before he left to take a shower.

Alex wondered why Roy had wanted to talk with the coaches. He didn't have to wait long. As soon as the morning practice was over and the boys had left for lunch, Coach Hanson approached Alex with one of the men from the Swimming Coaches Association.

"This is Coach Emerson from Victoria Park High," Coach Hanson introduced the white-haired man who had to be close to his retirement.

"You're doing a great job, young man," Coach Emerson said. "I just talked with one of your swimmers, and he literally praised you."

"You can't imagine how much I had to pay him for that," Alex said and grinned.

Coach Emerson gave him an odd look. Then the look of his eyes changed, and he burst out laughing.

"You study at Eastwood, right?" he said. "Victoria Park High is just a few blocks from the university."

Suddenly, Alex realized where this discussion was leading. His eyes opened wider, and he rapped his fingers lightly on his legs. *Please say it*, he thought and waited for the words to come out of the old man's mouth.

"I would like to offer you a job as an assistant coach," the old man said. "Assuming you're interested."

"For sure I am," Alex said quickly and offered his hand.

It took some time for Coach Emerson to understand that Alex wanted to shake hands with him. They did, and Alex kept thanking him over and over again.

When the coaches had left, Alex sat on the jumping stand. His body was shaking with excitement. He

185

wanted to call Liam, but his boyfriend was still in the hospital.

I love you so much, Alex thought and smiled alone in the empty swim hall.

The next surprise was waiting for Alex when he walked out of the swim hall after the afternoon practice. He glared at the boy who was leaning against the wall with a frightened look on his face.

"What are you doing here?" Alex asked Matthew.

"Please help me," Matthew said before pausing. "Could you please drive me to the rehab clinic?"

"You seriously want to get clean, don't you?"

Matthew nodded and looked at his toes. "I have nobody else to ask. I'm sure Liam doesn't want to see me," he said and added quickly, "and I don't blame him for that."

"Thanks to you, Liam is in the hospital," Alex said, "and I'm on my way there."

Slowly, Matthew turned and began walking away. His hair was messy, and his clothes were dirty. He must have spent the night out somewhere, probably hiding from his parents.

"Wait," Alex said.

After all, Matthew was, or had been, Liam's friend. Alex couldn't turn his back on him, no matter how much he wished he could.

"Let's take my car. I'll drive you there," he said.

At the same time, Roy walked out of the swim hall with Kevin. Roy saw Matthew and stopped.

"What is he doing here?" he asked and looked at Alex.

"It's okay," Alex said. "I'm taking him to the rehab clinic before I get Liam from the hospital."

"No. You'll go and see your boyfriend. Kevin and I can drive him there," Roy said and showed Alex the rope that he was carrying. "We're heading to Buonas anyway, and the clinic is on the way."

"Are you gonna tie me with that rope?" Matthew asked and took a step back.

"Only if you don't behave," Roy said and smirked. "Let's go."

Alex walked with the boys to the parking area, thanked Roy and Kevin for their help, and stepped into his Mustang. He had gotten a message from Liam that everything was okay, but he had to see his boyfriend with his own eyes.

The few miles from the high school to the hospital felt endless, like the road would never end. Finally, he made it there, parked his car, and rushed to the lobby where he found Liam sitting on a chair. He stood up and flashed a broad smile when he saw Alex.

Alex wrapped his arms around his boyfriend and squeezed him tight. "Oh God, I'm so happy you're okay," he said and planted a kiss on Liam's lips. He couldn't care less that the lobby was full of people.

"I need to … tell you something," Liam said, and his face grew severe.

"What is it?" Alex asked and took a half-step back.

"Let's talk in your car," Liam said.

Neither of them said anything while they walked to the parking area. Alex's mind was working in overdrive. Liam looked okay. What could possibly be wrong?

"What is it, honey?" Alex asked as soon as they were inside the car.

Liam just sat there turned toward him. His eyes were moving from side to side, but no words came out of his mouth.

"Is something wrong?" Alex asked, and the expression on his face would have turned more severe if it had been possible.

"I … I'm so sorry," Liam said. His eyes became moist, and he turned his head away.

What is this? Is he breaking up with me? Alex thought, confused, but he patted Liam gently on his shoulder.

"Tell me what's wrong. What are you sorry for?" Alex said softly.

Liam turned to look at him. "That I went to bed with Matthew," Liam blurted out, and tears fell down his cheeks.

"Oh, honey. It's not your fault," Alex said. He wrapped his arm around Liam and pulled his boyfriend as close to his chest as possible. "Matthew drugged you. Besides, you still had your clothes on when we arrived."

"Did I?"

"Don't you remember what happened?"

Liam shook his head. He leaned against Alex and let his boyfriend's arm stroke his upper body through his shirt. As he felt Liam began to relax, Alex pushed his hand under the shirt and touched Liam's soft skin.

"So, you still love me?" Liam said.

"Of course," Alex said and moved his hand to his boyfriend's crotch, where he found something hard bulging in his jeans. "And I can hardly wait until we get home."

Alex squeezed the notebook with both hands and followed how Roy turned at the end of the pool. The tall swimmer from Greenlands High in the adjacent lane was slightly ahead of him, but Roy still had a chance of winning if he had saved some energy for the final spurt.

"He's either first or second. The rest are too far from them," Luke said. He had been disqualified from the final and was standing next to Alex at the end of the lane.

There were lots of Fairmont High students and their parents in the audience, and the closer the swimmers got to the finish line, the louder the noise in the hall became.

Faster! You can make it, Alex thought and ground his teeth.

Roy and the other guy were only a few yards from the edge of the pool. The audience was standing, and everybody followed when the swimmers hit the touch pads. Alex turned to look at the monitor; Roy had won.

A moment later, Roy took off his goggles and looked at the monitor. With a broad smile on his face, he lifted his hand and almost hit the other swimmer who had come to congratulate him.

When Roy climbed out of the pool, Alex approached him and offered his hand. Roy ignored it and wrapped his wet arms around Alex.

"Thanks!" he said.

"Well, it was your accomplishment," Alex said.

Roy looked at him and pursed his lips. "We both know I was a dick, but you still gave me a chance," he said.

"We both know I like dick," Alex said, trying to keep his poker face.

Luke burst out laughing. Roy shook his head, but a small smile rose on his face. "You're testing my limits, Alex," he said and headed to the showers.

"I wish you were here coaching us next autumn," Luke said.

Alex knew that he wouldn't be. His place was with Liam in Eddington. They would have three more years before graduation, and now Alex had a job as well. He would coach high school kids, not here, but in Eddington.

"We still have two more days of swim camp. See you tomorrow in Buonas," Alex said.

The ceremony to award the winners would start soon, but he wanted to see Liam before that. He scanned the audience and found Liam sitting in his place at the end of the third row. Alex walked over to him and kissed Liam quickly on his cheek, ignoring some disapproving mutters from people nearby.

"You're a great coach," Liam said.

"Have I thanked you enough for the job?" Alex said and kissed Liam again, now on the lips.

"You did, yesterday." Liam grinned.

Alex's phone began to ring. It was the Athletics Director at Eastwood University. Alex listened carefully to what he had to say and promised to think about it before he hung up the phone.

"They offered me a place on the Eastwood swim team," Alex said. "The one that is vacant because…."

His words trailed off. Tyler's death was still too painful for him to want to mention it aloud, but maybe taking his place on the team was the best way to honor his friend's memory. It was probably what Tyler would have wanted.

"Of course you'll take it," Liam said and hugged Alex. "You've always been my swimmer boy."

Epilogue

4 YEARS AGO

Matthew sat next to Liam on the couch in the living room watching their favorite TV show. Even though their freshman year at school had just finished, he felt nervous. Liam was close to him—so close that, if he wanted, he could have touched him. And he did want to, but he didn't have courage.

What if he doesn't feel the same way? Matthew thought. *And what if what I feel is wrong?*

Not wanting to risk their friendship, Matthew moved his position on the couch. His hand touched Liam's thigh lightly, as if on accident. It wasn't, and Matthew watched closely how Liam would react. He didn't.

Was that a good sign? Maybe he liked it? Or maybe he didn't even notice, Matthew pondered and moved a bit closer to his friend. Liam turned to look at him and smiled.

"This is so funny," Liam said. "I wonder whether Mark will ever find his keys."

"Me, too," Matthew said, even though he wasn't sure what Liam meant. He hadn't been concentrating on the show.

Liam was still looking at him and was about to say something when Matthew couldn't resist it anymore. He leaned partly on top of Liam and began tickling his friend.

"Please … stop," Liam yelled, as much as he could from his giggling, and tried to tickle Matthew back.

Matthew couldn't help laughing when he felt Liam's fingers approaching his armpits. Being so close to his friend felt good, and he hoped they could be like this longer. Unfortunately, his mom interrupted it far too soon.

"Boys, behave!" she shouted from the kitchen.

"Yes, Mom," Matthew answered, disappointed.

He was even more disappointed when Liam fixed his position on the couch and left a clear gap between them. Sighing mentally, Matthew moved farther on his edge of the couch. They continued watching the show, which was okay, but not what he had wanted to do.

After the show ended, Liam left for home. It was already dinner time, and Matthew's mother had made it clear it would be a *family* dinner.

"See you tomorrow!" Matthew shouted after his friend.

Liam turned around in the yard, still the same smile on his face. "Sure! Let's take our bikes and ride somewhere."

Not knowing that the exchange was their final goodbye, Matthew walked to the kitchen and sat on the table. His sister was already there, and soon their father came from his study.

"Bow your heads," Mr. Evans said and continued with a loud, clear voice, "Lord, make us truly thankful for this food and all other blessings."

Matthew glanced at his sister, who was looking down with a severe expression on her face. *She's probably a better Christian than me*, he thought and shifted his focus back to his father's words.

"Teach us to know by whom we are fed. With bread of life our souls supply, that we may live with Christ on high," Mr. Evans finished the prayer.

"Amen," they all said and raised their heads.

A devout atmosphere filled the kitchen as the family enjoyed dinner, talking sparsely to each other. Matthew couldn't help thinking of Liam: his lean body, his black hair and brown eyes, and the smile on his cute face.

I wish he felt the same way as I do, Matthew thought. There was something special in their friendship, which made him hopeful. At the same time, he had nothing to compare since Liam was his only friend.

After dinner, Matthew helped his mother wash the dishes. She thought that the dishwasher was a luxury item and unnecessary flaunting. Besides, doing their share of the household work was the best way to teach Christian work ethics to her children.

When Matthew was drying the last plate, he accidentally dropped it on the floor. She gave him an angry glare and asked him to clean up the pieces. Obediently, Matthew opened the closet to get the broom and dustpan.

"Sorry, Mom. It was a mistake," he muttered.

"Is something wrong?" she asked after Matthew had collected the pieces. "You have been silent since Liam left. Did he hurt you?"

"No," Matthew said quickly. "It's not that."

"What is it then?" she said.

When Matthew didn't open his mouth to say anything, she asked him to join her in the living room. She closed the door so that they were alone. Then she sat next to her son on the couch and looked at him, demanding an answer. Matthew rubbed his fingers together and stared down.

"You're my son. You can tell me anything," Mrs. Evans said and fixed her blouse.

"Mom, I think I'm…." The words stuck in his throat, and he had to swallow before he continued. "I think I'm gay," he blurted out.

Her face grew severe. For a long time, she just stared at Matthew, who wished that she would say something. Anything would be better than the eerie silence that had filled the living room.

"You're not … homosexual," she said finally. "It's that boy who has made you believe such lies."

"Liam has done nothing. He doesn't even—" Matthew began.

"It's better you no longer see each other," she concluded and left the room.

Matthew watched as she disappeared into the kitchen. *This can't be true. She must be kidding*, he thought. Unfortunately, everybody who knew Mrs. Evans could tell that she seldom joked. If ever.

The following morning—grounded and in his room— Matthew heard his mother talking to Liam, who had come to see him. Her words made it clear that his worst nightmares had come true.

"Matthew is sick. Some bacteria, very contagious. He can't be in touch with anybody for at least two weeks," he heard her saying. Then she added, "It's better that you leave now."

School just ended! Will they keep me here as a prisoner the whole summer? Matthew thought. Luckily, one day, he had to go back to school. For the first time in his life, he wished that school would start again soon.

Matthew's imprisonment didn't last the entire summer. The next week, a big truck drove to their yard. Two men came out of the cab and began carrying their furniture to the truck.

"What's going on?" Matthew rushed to the kitchen and found his parents packing the tableware.

"Start packing your things. Take everything you want," his mother said. Her voice was as cold and calm as it had been since the discussion that had made him "sick."

"But why?"

"We're moving to Alabama."

His mouth wide open, he watched his parents, who continued packing their stuff, ignoring him completely. *This fucking can't be true*, Matthew thought. He rushed to his room and took the first thing he could find. It was the Carcassonne game that Liam had given him as a birthday present. His mind full of anger and frustration, he threw the game against the wall so hard that the box broke and the tiles flew all over his room.

"Matthew! Don't be childish. We're doing this for you," his mother shouted from the kitchen.

"You're ruining my life," Matthew cried. His voice was cracking.

Mrs. Evans walked to his room. "Don't you understand? We're saving you. I have arranged a good therapist for you there. He will help you with your problem," she said.

"I don't need a therapist. I just want to stay here," Matthew protested. He knew that now was not the right time to mention Liam's name.

"Start packing your things. We're leaving as soon as we're ready," she said.

"But—" Matthew began but stopped when he saw the expression on his mother's face.

It was too late. All decisions had been made for him. The only thing he could do was to take everything he wanted and pack it in the big cardboard box. Once everything was packed, the men came and took the box to the truck.

"Okay, let's go then," Mr. Evans said when the house was empty. "Matthew, Maria, go to the car."

"Can't I even go and tell Liam we're leaving?" Matthew asked.

His mother gave him a look that answered the question. "You heard what your father said."

His face in the backdoor window, Matthew watched as Liam's bedroom window disappeared behind the trees. He was sure he had seen Liam's face in the window. Tears streamed down his cheeks when he realized he might not see his friend ever again.

My life is over.

About the Author

Jay Argent is a novelist in his forties who lives a peaceful life with his husband. His favorite hobbies are music, movies, and romantic novels. He obtained a degree in engineering in 2001 and built a successful career in a management consulting firm. Using his own high school and college experiences as inspiration, he is now pursuing his true passion of writing.

If you have any feedback, you can contact him by email at jay@jayargent.com. He very much looks forward to hearing from you.

www.jayargent.com

Printed in Great Britain
by Amazon